TOMBSTONES AND TUMBLEWEED

TOMBSTONES AND TUMBLEWEED

•

EDNA VAN LEUVEN

AVALON BOOKS
THOMAS BOUREGY AND COMPANY, INC.
401 LAFAYETTE STREET
NEW YORK, NEW YORK 10003

PRINTED IN THE UNITED STATES OF AMERICA
ON ACID-FREE PAPER
BY HADDON CRAFTSMEN, SCRANTON, PENNSYLVANIA

To my darling Van

I have kept my promise

Chapter One—September 29, 1875

The wind was rising again. Agatha watched a dust devil twisting in the air as it skimmed across the ground. It picked up a brittle tumbleweed and discarded it beside an old tombstone, its inscription all but obliterated with age.

The soft voice of a mockingbird could be heard singing somewhere above in a cottonwood tree. At the back of the scattered group of mourners a baby was crying and people began to shuffle their feet, a few turning around. The child's mother soothed the tired infant and the crying stopped.

Even the horses seemed to be restless; Agatha watched as they flicked their tails to shoo away the bothersome flies. It was warm, unusually so for September, and ash from the fire just two days before seemed to cover everything left standing.

Agatha put her hand over her face in a futile effort to escape the strong, acrid odor. It was part of the very air they breathed and she wondered if it would ever go away.

Sounds from one of the saloons that had survived the disaster drifted down toward the cemetery: a woman's shrill laugh, a curse, the rattle of bar glasses. A creaking wagon moved slowly down Virginia City's main street just above the cemetery. Men were already busy pulling down what was left of St. Paul's Episcopal Church not too far away. The air was filled with the echoes of a devastated town clearing away the burned and battered buildings; the townspeople were still burying their dead.

Vicar Johnson stood before the grave. Agatha looked at him through veiled eyes. He seemed so frail and vulnerable. She wondered if what had happened to his parishioners had been too much for this temperate man of God. His thin shoulder blades showed clearly through his worn alpaca coat, and gentle wisps of white hair seemed to sit like cotton tufts around his neck and across his pale, pink scalp. Beads of sweat trickled down his flushed face. His knuckled fingers held tightly to the Bible as he spoke; Agatha wanted somehow to comfort him.

"Man that is born of woman hath but a short time to live and is full of misery. He cometh up and is cut down like a flower."

Agatha stood beside the grave. Dust from the fire continued to make it difficult to breathe, and her black bombazine mourning dress felt too heavy, its high collar tight about her neck. It was impossible to bend in prayer as the vicar spoke a final word. She knew people were watching but she could not, would not pretend that she was grieving. Still, she was thankful for the heavy veil covering her face. It did not matter in the least that her eyes were dry. Her friends, people who had come out of respect for her, not for Jonathan, would understand.

Two grave diggers stood a respectable distance away, one leaning on the handle of his shovel, waiting. He was wearing a faded, soiled shirt that was soaked with sweat, the sleeves rolled up above his elbows. The other man lifted off his shabby hat and with a rag dried the inside of the moist crown and placed it back on his head. His impatience showed.

Agatha was watching them, her mind wandering while trying not to think about herself and her real grief. Not for this man, never for that.

Someone took Agatha's arm with a steady grip. The touch brought her back to the present. She was led forward and handed a flower. She wondered where someone had found such a beautiful rose in a town that had all but burned to the ground. That such a thought should come into her mind at such a moment struck Agatha as ludicrous and out of place. But then, all that had been happening was in itself ludicrous and out of place. She dropped the flower on the casket, not wanting even to touch the wood, and then waited until the others had said their condolences and had moved gratefully away.

There was no one near enough to hear her last words.

"Good-bye, Jonathan. May God have mercy on your evil soul."

Nate stood patiently by the surrey, his shoulders bent, his sparse, graying hair blowing slightly in a sudden rush of wind. A storm was growing over the mountains to the west and the air was chilling quickly. The bright yellow sky was swallowed up by clouds, and the black debris that filled the air was caught up in a sudden gush of the western wind. A gray gauze seemed to cover everything.

He looked up as Agatha came forward; his eyes misted and his sun-browned face became a crisscross pattern of wrinkles as he watched her walking toward him. He pulled his hat down tightly on his head against the strong wind, then reached to help her. She hesitated only a moment, took a deep breath, and stepped up into the surrey.

Nate went around the other side and climbed up into the driver's seat just as another gush of wind caused the horses to shy. His strong, weathered hands grabbed the reins and they became quiet again.

The sky had turned a deeper shade of gray and the storm began in earnest; now it started to rain.

Agatha turned and looked back one last time as a flash of lightning brought everything into focus. The casket had been lowered and the workmen were hastily shoveling dirt to cover it. She pulled her shawl around her body and shivered violently, remembering Jonathan Woodrow.

Just below the cemetery George Trentwell stood looking out the blackened window frame of Trentwell's Saloon and Gambling Establishment, his elbows deep within the black ash that covered the sill. He could see clearly, from his vantage point, the wagons and horses moving away from Boot Hill as they headed home, if indeed any had homes to go to. Some of those at the funeral would be traveling all the way to Gold Hill or Carson City to stay with family or friends, for their own homes had been destroyed and their lives were in ruin. Others, mostly cowpokes and Chinese workmen from the railroad, would be staying in hastily erected campsites, hoping that the tents and wooden shacks would be sufficient for temporary living quarters until Virginia City could rise from the ashes, if indeed it ever did.

He turned and looked at what was left of his saloon. Half the roof was gone, what remained was covered by a makeshift tarp that wasn't going to stand the strain of bad weather. The bar, which through some magical whim of the fire had survived unmarred, stood with its mahogany surface now clean and shining again, a ludicrous remnant of the town's previous life standing out in the carnage. It was surrounded with people sitting on bar stools that should, or could, at any moment collapse, for unlike the bar most had not escaped damage. The entire building was crowded with people usually loud and boisterous, but now quiet—too quiet. Each man and woman seemed to be living in their own private world of wonder and disbelief—wonder that they had even survived and disbelief that the devastation had ever happened.

George looked back again at the scene below. He could see Agatha's surrey heading out of town toward the ranch. The horses were a fleeting blur of distorted motion through the cracked and broken window, but he could see clearly Agatha's black figure sitting ramrod straight, her head high, seemingly unaware of the wind and the rain that swirled around her head. He marveled at this magnificent young woman who had borne so much pain, so much sorrow with such grace and dignity. He sighed audibly.

The air seemed colder somehow. Rain began to drum against the grimy window with a staccato beat. Rivulets of dirt ran slowly down the window in uneven, ugly streaks. The storm was hitting with full force now. The rain began in earnest, cold and sharp, with stinging drops that quickly soaked into the powdery earth and intensified the smoldering odor of the fire. If the rain came on hard enough the makeshift roof would collapse. The owner of Trentwell's Saloon and Gambling Establishment could only turn away. There was nothing else he could do.

Lizbeth Roberts had been Agatha's friend since the two of them had been in school together. She stood now on the front porch of the hospital, one of the few buildings still standing, her baby in her arms and young Bobby clinging to her, his tiny arms wrapped around her knees. Off in the distance she could see the mourners leaving the cemetery. She had wanted so to be there, but it was impossible with her husband still recovering from his fall while helping fight the fire. The children were still withdrawn and frightened. And so was Lizbeth. Not for herself—she always managed to land on her feet—but for her best friend. Agatha seemed to be holding up, (at least she was keeping up appearances), but Lizbeth knew better. Nobody could be that brave all the time and keep on going.

"Mama, please, can we go inside?"

The words were from Jennifer, her oldest, just ten and already so grown up. The tragedy had made all of them seem to grow up too quickly; they weren't acting the way children should act. Lizbeth looked at Jennifer, at her tiny solemn face; it just wasn't right that she should look like that, she was just a little girl.

"Mama, it's cold and it's raining!"

Only then did Lizbeth realize that the cemetery was empty. She could see the surrey going up the hill toward the Manor. And it was cold, God it was cold!

Nate rode the team home slowly; the horses were anxious, the reins tight within his grasp to keep them from becoming uncontrollable again as the wind whipped through the trees. The last stretch on the long hill past town lay ahead. Agatha was glad to feel the road level and knew that home was not too far away. Ahead she could see the outline of Brunswick Manor. A light was coming from the kitchen window; it flickered as the shutters rattled in the wind and Agatha caught a glimpse of Clarisa, her outline a thin silhouette within the window frame, watching for them. It was only then she realized that the night had turned cold, the kind of sudden, bone-chilling cold that comes on so quickly in the high desert.

Clarisa leaned against the sink and stared down at the pile of heavy china dishes. A fly landed on the water and she slapped impatiently at it with her hand. It splattered water everywhere. She stood for a moment looking down, trying not to think about the pain that had been part of all of their lives for much too long a time.

Reaching elbow deep into the water, she began again to rub the bar of brown soap she was holding too tightly. She scrubbed with quick, violent motions, the strength in her thin-fingered hands a surprising gesture for this wisp of a woman who looked as delicate as silk. Everyone who knew her understood that she was a tough one.

A heavy gust of wind slammed against the kitchen window. Until that moment Clarisa had not noticed the black sky.

"A black storm for a black day." She spoke out loud, the words an anxious sound from the back of her throat.

She looked again. The surrey was coming through the gates. Agatha would need her. Drying her hands on her muslin apron, she rushed down the hallway to open the main door, her body shivering in the sudden burst of chill air. The two friends didn't need words. Agatha removed her hat and placed it on the halltree in the entryway, not noticing the rain that dripped from its brim. Standing at the doorway to the parlor, she hesitated, looked down at her damp clothing, and with the side of her hand brushed at the rain that was clinging to the black cloth. It was an empty gesture. Clarisa stood quietly for a moment, then left to return a few moments later with a mug of hot chocolate. Agatha was standing alone by the empty fireplace.

"You drink this now, ya hear me?" Clarisa spoke quietly. She ached to hold Agatha and comfort her, but knew that nothing would help, not yet.

Nate still stood off to one side of the entry with his hat in his hands; Clarisa saw his chest swell as he sucked in a tight breath and then exhaled with a heavy sigh. He could only stand and shake his head. There was so little anyone could do.

"Come on, Clarisa, you can give me some of that chocolate too. Let's go into the kitchen."

Clarisa looked again at Agatha standing by the mantel and let Nate take her by the hand and walk out of the room, down the stillness of the empty hall and into the kitchen.

"Darn it, darn it, darn it!"

"Clarisa, don't! It won't do any good. It's all over. She will be fine and so will we, you just wait and see, my girl."

"I just couldn't go with her, Nate. I tried. God knows I tried, but I couldn't stand to be that close to that man, even dead! Look what he did to us all—none of us will ever be the same again. And look at her. . . ."

The sentence was never finished. Clarisa pulled up

her apron and began to cry in deep sobs. Nate put his arms around her and held her until the crying stopped.

Inside the parlor the slow ticking of the clock on the mantel could be heard, its pendulum beating off the seconds in the silent room. The sounds of the storm were only an echo as it moved away up into the hills.

Agatha stood alone by the empty fireplace, her thoughts on all that had happened these past seven months. First Lucas had disappeared, then her father had died, and today she had had to go through this travesty. She was alone. She walked to the window, opened it, and pushed aside the shutters. The storm was increasing again, with flashes of lightning that danced across the desert illuminating the Virginia Mountains and the valley below. Closing the window, she could see her own haunted reflection looking back from the glass. She could not imagine how a man like Lucas Forester could have found her, plain Agatha Brunswick, attractive. What had happened to him, to their plans, to their love?

"Where are you, Lucas, where are you?"

With those words spoken she turned her back to the reflection in the window, as if in doing so the very gesture would obliterate the memory of these past months.

Clarisa came back into the room.

"You want anything else, dear?" the little house-keeper said, concern filling her voice.

"No, I'm all right. I'll finish my chocolate and go up to bed."

"You need me, child, you just call. I won't be able

to sleep tonight anyway.'' She hesitated, then continued, ''You hear me now? I'm close if there's cause.''

Clarisa watched for a moment, turned, and left. Agatha finished her drink and looked around this familiar room where she had spent so much of her life, where so much had been said—words of love, words of hate, and one horrible moment with her father that had all but obliterated reason. Then, putting down her empty cup, she walked silently out into the hall, up the dark, circular staircase and into her room. She stood looking at the shadows that filled the room and thought again about Lucas; the memory of him was like a shadow that followed her everywhere. Even through the darkest of nights, where in black stillness no shadows dwell, she could still feel his presence. There would never, ever be another moment when that undulating, elusive, but ever-present shadow would not be there.

She found herself still standing in the middle of the empty room and wondered how long she had been there. A flash of lightning drew her to the window. Below the town still smoldered and puffs of steam were rising from the ashes. She stood for a long time looking up into the clouds. The storm was moving away again toward the east, leaving behind it an unsettling quiet.

All that could be heard was a soft rain whispering through the night air.

Chapter Two—March 1875

The train ride into Virginia City seemed to take forever. Lucas Forester could feel the grit between his teeth from the black smoke that was belching out of the locomotive's smokestack. It was a long, tiring trip from Kansas City. He would be glad to see the inside of a hotel room and feel the warmth of a bath and the comfort of clean clothes. A shave would be nice too.

Outside, the desert blooms shone with the brilliance of spring, the sand shimmered a warm shade of pink, and the mountains were green with sage and tumbleweed. Lucas was always surprised at the colors in this part of the country and the deep valleys with their rolling terrain. Snow still clung to the peaks of the higher mountains—it would be weeks before it would melt and disappear. He had expected to find the Nevada desert to be more like the Sahara, flat and monotonous. It was anything but that.

Ranches were coming into view, hidden behind shadows, with only fences and an occasional chimney to give away their presence. Cattle could be seen grazing, too busy to even notice the iron monster moving across the almost empty space. Now and again a lone rider would lift a hat and wave toward strangers riding past in dusty coaches, only their heads and shoulders showing through square windows. A train was a noisy interruption in this lonely country.

Lucas waved back at one old cowboy who, when he waved, sent a cloud of dust through the air from his old and battered hat. He watched another who sat tall and straight, motionless as a hitching post. Beside him his horse grazed quietly in a stand of warm grass. The horse lifted its head for a moment, then went back to eating. Lucas could see it twitching its nostrils as it enjoyed the small, lush stand of green. The cowboy simply ignored the passing train.

When the conductor opened the Pullman door, waves of hot air, dust, and even more black soot from the locomotive rushed in. People looked up at the interruption and began to move around, arms stretching, legs shuffling; these were tired, uncomfortable people, all waiting for the long trip to end.

Lucas looked to his right and saw the Truckee River shimmering in the sunlight—another desert surprise. Along the riverbank trees flourished and grew as the sparkling, cold waters from the mountains above moved down the hillsides and through the valleys.

Another hour and the train would be pulling into the station at Virginia City. Lucas stood and walked toward the end of the car. Some company and a cool drink would help pass the time, and the club car was only one car away. The air outside was just as hot as inside, but the breeze felt good as he moved forward. Opening the second door, he could see the same three passengers that had been there hours before: two businessmen who looked like salesmen, and a woman whose occupation could be anything. She sat alone, a plain, dour-faced woman in a dress that had seen better days and a hat with a lone, bedraggled rose stuck unceremoniously on its crown. She spoke to no one, only stared out the smoky window at the endless expanse. It was obvious that she did not see anything outside.

"Hi, gentleman . . . and lady." Lucas, always polite, had added the latter. The quiet woman ignored him.

"Come to join us again, have you, sir?" one of the salesmen said. His face was flushed and sweating from, Lucas imagined, a combination of the heat, the high starched collar of his shirt (now wilted and stained), and too much drinking.

The second man half-rose, grinned faintly, and lurched back down into his seat unsteadily as the train turned a curve. He looked as tired as Lucas felt. These three occupants of the club car were not going to be the stimulating company he needed, but the bartender, a tall, thin black man, might be. He smiled at Lucas and motioned toward a seat at the far end of the bar.

''Been a long day,'' he spoke aloud to the barman.

''Has been that, sir,'' the barman answered as he nodded toward the three who were now ignoring the new arrival.

The tall barman and Lucas talked awhile about things in general while Lucas drank a tall bourbon and water, and then he left, unnoticed by the others, to return to his seat by the window to think about the reason for his journey—the chance to buy a ranch close to Virginia City, a chance at a new kind of life away from Kansas City and the complex problem that had seemed lately to plague his life. He wanted no part of where that was leading, although he knew in his heart that there was a solution, a very simple one, but one he had tried to avoid. People would be hurt, people he cared about, but the whole thing had not been his fault and it made him furious to reason that, while he had not caused the problem, he would most certainly have to be the one to make the decision to bring the whole thing out in the open and end it, once and for all. Just thinking about Connie and her mother made him angry again, angry not only at the problem—at who was causing it—but more than anything else angry at himself for putting off what he knew he must someday do. He wondered, not for the first time, if he should broach the subject with Conrad, who was also looking into the matter of purchasing the Brunswick ranch and would no doubt be at the meeting with the owner, Hiram Brunswick. And Conrad was, after all, Connie's father. Procrastinating only made him angrier at himself. He had never been a man to put off a job, however unpleasant—until now.

The man sitting across from Lucas looked his way.

"Did you say something, sir?"

Only then did he realize that he had been talking to himself. Embarrassed, he dropped his chin down to his chest and shook his head.

"Sorry, just talking out loud."

"I understand, sir, I do it myself all the time. Silly habit, isn't it?"

Lucas nodded in agreement and returned to his own thoughts.

But he knew he would remain silent in Conrad's company. He would have to handle this face-to-face with Connie. Talking to Conrad would be cowardice. That wasn't his style either.

The train was slowing down. Lucas had been too wrapped up in his thoughts to notice that the train was pulling into the station. For now the problem in Kansas City would have to wait.

At last Lucas found himself standing on the train platform. He stepped down into the brilliant sunshine and smiled. The sunlight was a blinding contrast to the dark train interior. Lucas pulled the brim of his hat down farther on his forehead and, squinting, looked toward town. Crossing the dusty street was a short man in a long, dark shirt and trousers shuffling in tiny, chopped steps behind the cart he was pushing. He had a black pigtail down his back, and it was then that

Lucas realized the man was Chinese. The man disappeared down an alley and out of sight.

Lucas started walking over the platform and toward the sidewalk. He was surprised to see that it was made out of wooden boards. Stepping up, he almost collided with a tiny girl with smiling green eyes whose red curls were bouncing playfully above a cherubic face covered with freckles.

"Young lady, would you please direct me to the hotel."

"That way, mister." She pointed and continued running.

Lucas picked up his valise and headed down the street.

Hiram Brunswick was a tall man, solidly built, with wavy brown hair just beginning to turn gray. He wore a full mustache and a beard that covered his very square jaw. His green eyes glistened when he was amused— which was seldom—and turned to stone when he was angry. He was rather cold and unresponsive, exuding an air of untouchability. For the most part people in town had learned to accept Hiram's aloofness. He was, after all, the president of the Virginia Bank.

Agatha had never questioned her father's actions; of her mother she knew very little except that she had died when Agatha was only three. A shimmering memory of a sweet lady who left the scent of lavender was all that remained.

The two people closest to Agatha were Clarisa, the housekeeper for Brunswick Manor, and Nate, the foreman who handled things at the ranch. They had both been part of the family for most of her life.

Clarisa was fair but uncompromising. Her frail frame made her seem brittle, but nothing was further from the truth. She had a warm and caring heart—she simply did not display her emotions and loyalties to the world.

Nathan P. Culpepper—Nate, as he liked to be called—had come to them a half-starved cowboy really down on his luck. He had quit a big outfit that, as he said, didn't exactly do things according to the Good Book. To his credit he had never told anyone just what it was they had done, just that he wanted no part of doing wrong by your neighbor.

March was an unpredictable month on the desert. The wind could rise, sliding across the Sierra Nevada without warning, and bring with it sandstorms, clouds, rain, or even hailstones. It could stop as quickly as it had started, leaving the desert glowing with sunshine.

This day had brought with it skies so clear and blue Nate had to squint against the glare. It was time to take the boss down to the bank.

The surrey stood at the front veranda, Nate waiting patiently as he did every morning. It was quiet on the ranch; the hands were busy fixing fences where a wild herd of horses had slipped through and torn away some of the older fence posts at the south end of the ranch. Clarisa could be heard bustling around in the kitchen. Nate smiled. Clarisa was never quiet about anything she did. But the whole household was alive with activity. Part of the ranch was for sale, and several prospective buyers and friends were coming to dinner. It was going to be a very active day, and Nate knew that Clarisa would be banging pots and pans around for hours.

"Beautiful day!" Nate spoke as they rode over the crooked road leading down into Virginia City.

"Yes, Nate, it is that," Hiram replied, but his mind was on the meeting ahead.

"Those cattlemen coming to dinner tonight, you think one of them might buy the land?"

"If they talk the right price, and then you can get that spread at Gold City. But remember, Nate, I can still use you at the ranch; we will be keeping twenty acres. There will always be the horses and the regular maintenance. You're needed, you know that."

"Oh, yes sir. All I'm waitin' for is trying to get up enough nerve to ask a certain somebody to marry me! A lot will depend on that."

Hiram smiled. He knew, as did everybody in town, that Nate wanted to marry Clarisa. Clarisa seemed to be the only one that was unaware of this deep devotion.

The sun was rising over the mountains as the ever-changing shadows of the higher hills moved their quiet dance across the road. Hiram still wondered at the absolute difference between Virginia City and where he had been born and lived for so long a time. The little house on Arch Street seemed very far away—never quite far enough, but as far as he had been able to go all those years ago.

The sound of people clumping down the wooden walks mingled with that of moving horses and barking dogs greeted Hiram as he walked past two young men perched on the front steps of his bank. He greeted them with a nod of his head, went through the door, and headed to the back of the building and his private office. Several people smiled good morning, and his head teller, Victor, left his desk and followed Hiram into the office.

"They're here and will probably be late from what I heard happened last night. They had themselves a time at the Bucket of Blood—seems Matty had her hands full. No trouble, just three thirsty men letting off steam. They're staying at Mrs. Hoffman's board-inghouse down on Second Street. Want me to go shake them loose?"

Victor stood waiting for an answer with his hands folded over his ample stomach, fingers fumbling and twisting a key chain that was suspended over his vest. He was a very short man with black hair that he combed over his balding head in an unsuccessful attempt at concealment; his booming, deliberate tone commanded attention. He was Hiram's right hand and as loyal as any son might have been.

"No, Victor, they'll wander in. I don't want to seem too anxious. They're coming to dinner tonight. I want you to be there. Think Marjorie will mind? Sorry, I meant to ask you earlier."

He stood erect and answered. "Certainly. Figured as much. I've already told the missus." Hiram nodded.

"Good, I really do want your input. We'll probably have a late poker game, but you don't have to stay for that if you don't care to."

"Probably not. I never win anyway." He smiled.

Victor left to return to the front of the bank; he was looking forward to this evening. Brunswick Manor was always a pleasant place to visit; Agatha was a wonderful hostess and Clarisa a marvelous cook. Marjorie, he thought, could take lessons from Clarisa. He smiled to himself. He loved Marjorie, who was a sweet and loving woman, but a cook—never! It hadn't mattered. Victor had been a bachelor for most of his adult life, and the miracle of finding someone who cared for him as much as Marjorie did was enough for him. As he walked back toward his office he remembered the first time he had seen her, a tiny little thing standing at a teller window. His life had never been the same. A wonderful wife and a position that he enjoyed—he was a complete and happy man.

There was something unusually beautiful about this morning, Agatha was thinking as she stood looking out the parlor window. An apricot sun was rising over the meadows to the east. Shimmering mist had formed soft halos around the sage still cool from the lingering night air, and a few clouds were still clinging to the white-capped mountain peaks.

Leaving the room, she headed back to the kitchen. "Clarisa, any coffee left?"

"For you, you bet!"

The two sat in the huge ranch kitchen drinking their coffee; they both knew how busy the day was going to be and this one quiet moment, before they started, would be the last of the day.

"Lordy, I hate thinking about tonight. All those big

cigar-smokin' men and you. I sure hope they watch their language. Do you remember that bunch your dad had in from Carson City? Last November, seems like. Anyway, their language was awful!

"They gonna' play poker too?" She added.

Agatha sighed and smiled, then leaned over and patted Clarisa's hand.

"Father didn't say, but let's be prepared for anything. Now, what's for dinner and how can I help?"

"Well, there's roast beef, mashed white potatoes, creamed onions, carrots, and coleslaw. I made a couple of apple pies early on. And I think I got me enough peas from the early garden for somethin' green."

Clarisa kept on talking about the dinner while Agatha listened and watched the sun rising higher into the morning sky. It was going to be a glorious day.

Suddenly the door from the pantry opened and Nate came bustling in eating one of Clarisa's homemade doughnuts.

"You comin' in through that pantry again, you scoundrel!" Clarisa scolded. Picking up a wooden spoon, she started after him.

"How many times I gotta' tell you not to steal my doughnuts! You ornery cuss, get outa my kitchen!"

"Now, Clarisa, you just behave, woman! You know how much I love your cookin'!" Nate tried talking, eating, and all the time dancing around the room while Clarisa, wooden spoon in hand, came after him.

"Enough, you two!" Agatha was laughing.

Nate ran back out the way he came in and grabbed another doughnut for good measure.

Clarisa put down the spoon, lifted up her huge white apron, and mopped at her flushed face. She was chuckling.

"That damned man will be the death of me yet!"

"Let's get busy, there's a lot to do," Agatha said as she looked out again through the window at the shimmering landscape.

Most people would look at her as a spinster, twenty-four and still unmarried, but Agatha thought little about it and had accepted her life in this remote mining town as her duty to her father. She had always been content. There had never been a serious beau in her life. Many men were intimidated by her father, his position, and his brittle ways. Agatha seemed not to notice.

"I wonder if I have spring fever?" Agatha asked out loud.

"What's that you said, honey?"

"I was wondering if I have spring fever. I feel so good today, maybe it's the beautiful sunrise. It's like you felt on Christmas morning as a child. There seems to be an excitement in the air. Whatever it is, I just plain feel good today."

Walking outside to enjoy the gentle touch of the desert morning, she thought again about how she felt and wondered why. Perhaps it was spring fever or maybe just the perfume of the desert air and the carpet of sunshine that covered the yard. The hollows between the mountain peaks had turned a deep plum where the shadows formed on the western curve, and below the valley changed color as the sun moved slowly through the day. Agatha wondered again why she felt this pleasant glow.

"It is just a nice day. Or perhaps it is simply this wonderful weather."

It wasn't either one.

Chapter Three

Noise from the wheels of a milk wagon, clattering over the cobblestones on Broad Street, woke Jonathan. He cursed aloud and for a moment thought about trying to go back to sleep, then he remembered. This was the beginning of his last day working in Philadelphia. By this time next week he would be in Kansas City and beginning a whole new career. No more accounting, no more bankers, no more putting up with Jones and Company, Bank Examiners. He was at last going to do what he had always wanted to do—he was going to go into the detective business. This was something he had wanted to do ever since his Uncle Samuel had been to visit him years before—how many years ago had that been? He couldn't remember exactly, a good twenty, at least. It had been when Jonathan was first employed at Jones and Company, still young and impressionable, but something he had never forgotten, a dream he had never dismissed or ignored. All these years he had remembered and planned and hoped. Now at last he was going to be a part of his uncle's firm. His chance had finally come, and under the very best of conditions. His uncle, a bachelor, had died and left the entire business to him.

Jonathan jumped out of bed, did a jig around the room, poured water into a basin and splashed his face, grabbed a towel to dry, and danced another jig. He would be leaving this gloomy boardinghouse and starting a whole new life.

The other boarders were already eating when he arrived at the table. Mrs. Jones was coming in from the kitchen with a second platter of eggs and stopped for a moment as she noticed Jonathan sliding back his chair. She seemed about to speak, thought better of it, and put the dish down on the table. It landed with a heavy thump!

"The eggs are warm, the rest of breakfast will probably be a little cold for you, Mr. Woodrow. I will get you some hot coffee. The second pot isn't quite ready. You will simply have to wait until it is done!"

The coolness in her voice was enough for them all to understand her meaning. Mrs. Jones ran a strict boardinghouse.

Jonathan smiled at everyone as he sat down on the hard, thin-backed oak chair, and received nothing but stares in return. He didn't care. His valise was ready to go and so was he.

All he could think of now was the future—so long

to the boarders at Broad and Girard Streets, Philadelphia, Pennsylvania! Inside he was bubbling. Look out, Kansas City, here comes Jonathan Woodrow!

The air inside the building on Walnut Street was stifling! Jonathan wondered if it was this humid in Kansas City. He doubted it. Nothing could be worse than the humidity on the East Coast—at least that is what everybody said.

Miss Morgenthal, from her desk across the room, tilted her head down and peered over her glasses, which sat perpetually on the tip of her rather large nose. Jonathan wondered why they never fell off. He smiled at her as he continued pulling his arms out of the sleeves of his coat and placed it limply over the back of his chair. Just let anybody say anything at all in this dreadful heat. One word and he would be out the door like a shot. He had to smile. He could feel her eyes on his back, and the whole office could hear her clearing her throat, a loud offensive sound, her way of showing her disapproval. Jonathan's smile became a full-throated laugh.

It was much later. The office had given him a going away party of sorts—if you could call a cake and warm lemonade a party. He had been disgusted with the whole thing but thinking back now he was glad that he had been polite. One never knew when one might need former associates—especially in his new business. Bank examiners were, in their own way, detectives after all, or so Jonathan decided as he sat in his own compartment on the train heading west. He was at last shaking off the dust of the past and heading toward a prosperous future.

Jonathan sipped at his drink, glanced at his watch, looked out the window, and then down at his toes that rested comfortably on the opposite, unoccupied seat. The private opulence had him heady with self-importance.

"Now, this is the life!"

Why not? he thought. His future was secure; why should he sit in a Pullman car and put up with stuffy people, sniveling children who always managed to put their feet up on the back of your seat and push? Why should he have to wear a coat in this heat? Wouldn't Miss Morgenthal enjoy seeing him like this! Jonathan laughed out loud and sipped again at his cool drink. This was great! He looked out at the passing scenery. Pennsylvania was a beautiful state with softly rolling green hills. He wondered what it would be like in Kansas City.

He slid down in his seat and, pushing his feet forward, wiggled his toes on the back of the dark plush, plum-colored mohair of the seat across from him.

He thought again, *My own compartment, my own seat, my own cool drink, my own business. Wow!*

Conrad Fillmore was sick of listening to the women chattering. Usually he could turn off the sound by simply sitting down and reading his paper. Tonight it didn't seem to help. His wife and daughter were entertaining friends and playing whist. The racket that four women could make was worse than a herd of cattle. Conrad wondered, not for the first time, why he, a cattleman, had married a woman from the city who was more interested in the latest fashions from Paris than in the cattle business. She should have been! It was what kept the family accepted in the best circles of society. At least in Kansas City circles. The compromise had been long in coming. They lived in town, but Conrad's business took him all over the country. It suited him fine. He wondered what they would think if he decided to buy the property in Virginia City and insisted they move west.

Now that was a scene to conjure up!

He slammed down his newspaper and walked out to the back veranda, whiskey in hand, and looked up at the stars. It was one beautiful night, cooler than it had been for days. He hoped it wouldn't be hot again tomorrow when the train arrived.

The train station in Kansas City was overcrowded, even for a business day when people were commuting home from work. With the heat as bad as it was Conrad wondered how much longer he would have to wait for that damned detective to arrive from Philadelphia. As much as he hated starting all over again with his investigation of the real worth of Hiram Brunswick, the thought of going to yet another agency was out of the question. At least this new man would have all the facts as presented to the previous owner of Woodrow Detective Agency, who had, unfortunately, died. All he could hope for was that the new man was not an incompetent fool; there were a lot of questions to be answered. Conrad had no intention of buying a ranch in Nevada without a lot of answers, although to be honest he hadn't known Hiram that long. What bothered him more than anything was the fact that he knew nothing of the man's past. Everybody had a past. Everybody that Conrad knew had one, except Hiram Brunswick of Virginia City. And Conrad was a very cautious man when it came to his money.

The heat was becoming more intense as more and more people waited for the train from New York and Philadelphia. Conrad reached up inside his collar and wiped away the sweat that was running down his face and staining his shirt.

"Darn it, where is that train? It's already ten minutes late."

He spoke to no one in particular, but a few people turned and smiled. No one else had spoken, but all of them were annoyed.

It didn't help. The train was still late.

Jonathan woke with a start. He groped for his glasses and fumbled for his watch stuck in the pocket of his trousers draped across the bottom of the berth.

"Oh, my God!" he exclaimed, looking at the time. The train would be pulling into Kansas City in half an hour. He would barely have time to shave and get dressed. His head was splitting. He groaned loudly as he tried to put his foot through a trouser leg as the train rolled from side to side. Usually it wouldn't have mattered how he looked but he was meeting his first client at the station and now, he knew, he would look anything but his best. Twenty minutes later, dressed and haphazardly shaved, he heard the conductor.

"Kansas City, Kansas City, ten minutes to Kansas City."

Jonathan opened the compartment door and shouted, "Get me some coffee, coffee! I have to have some coffee! And I mean now!"

His exclamation was loud and very much to the point.

The conductor looked up, surprised. There were a lot of people traveling who were rude, but this was even a little too much. He smiled nonetheless. It was his job.

"I'll see what I can do, sir, but we are almost into the station."

"I don't give a hoot if the president is meeting us— get me a cup of coffee!"

The conductor smiled again and turned away, but his smile disappeared as quickly as it had come. He swore under his breath and headed for the dining car.

"Darn troublemaker!" he exclaimed as the door to the car closed. "Every trip there just has to be one troublemaker and he has to be mine!"

Conrad Fillmore and Jonathan Woodrow were sitting in a private room at Delancey's. They were just about finished with their lunch. The room was small and decorated with heavy, dark walnut furniture. It fit Conrad Fillmore's idea of a perfect room for fine food and business. He liked to be quiet while he ate and needed privacy for any business dealings. Trying to get either one at home was an absolute impossibility. After losing his patience once too often because of Connie and her friends at home, he had made arrangements at Delancey's to have a private room available at a moment's notice. This was one of those times. There would be a great deal of money and a dramatic change in his life if he decided to buy the ranch Hiram Brunswick had for sale. He had to be certain of every detail. It would be to his advantage to know all about the man's private life as well as the value of the property. If he was going to have the upper hand he would need all the facts pertaining to the seller. This was especially true when he knew there would be other potential buyers at the meeting with the seller in Virginia City.

Conrad Fillmore was nobody's fool!

They were finally through eating. Conrad offered his guest a cigar, which he accepted. They pushed back their chairs simultaneously and sat quietly enjoying the tobacco. Conrad relaxed but did not move his eyes away from Jonathan, sizing up this man across the table from him. Jonathan was doing the same but without as much intensity.

"Jonathan, how about a little cognac? It helps the digestion."

Jonathan blew a puff of smoke toward the ceiling. He took his time in answering. He was sitting with one leg crossed over the other, his left hand in his watch pocket, the other holding his Havana. He was not in any hurry to answer. He changed the crossed legs from one to the other.

"Sounds good to me."

Conrad got up from his chair and opened the outer door. He spoke to someone who must have been just outside. He ordered, then shut the door and stood quietly for a moment before he sat down again. He wanted to get another good look at his guest.

Jonathan Woodrow was short, not over five foot six, with very dark eyes that always seemed to be squinting. His hair was a muddy brown. He needed a haircut badly and it was obvious that his last shave had been hastily accomplished. A paunch hung over his belt, and his short legs gave him the appearance of a gnome. His huge hands looked strong enough to choke a man with ease. His voice was the first thing that Conrad had noticed; it was a high-pitched tenor that grated on the nerves. Conrad didn't like Jonathan and hadn't liked his uncle, but sometimes it was better this way—it kept a man on guard. His uncle had been an unscrupulous detective but the best in his field. You didn't necessarily need to like a man to use him.

"Your uncle did all kinds of investigating. I understand you were into some type of investigating—bank accounts, that sort of thing. Am I right?"

Just then the waiter came with their brandy and conversation stopped. Jonathan watched as the glasses were placed on the table and the waiter left. Only then did he answer.

"Let me put it this way. I always did whatever was needed to obtain information about the people involved in what turned out to be, a lot of times, bank fraud. You would be amazed at how many ways people can steal from a bank.''

Conrad looked down into his glass and swirled the brandy in his glass. The cognac left a smooth, shiny trace around the sides of the snifter. He lifted it to his nostrils and drew in a whiff of the aroma. Only then did he lift it to his lips and sip. It burned pleasantly down his throat. Jonathan took a large swallow of his brandy and Conrad watched as the rather uncouth man's face turned red.

Jonathan coughed a bit, reached up with his empty hand and ran his fingers around the front of his too-warm collar. ''I look into people's background, you know, their resources, family, contacts, whatever a client requires. Nothing illegal, mind you, but sometimes a businessman needs to know more about the people he associates with than can be seen on the surface. It takes a lot of digging, you can be sure of that. Everybody, and I mean everybody, has something to hide. I pride myself in finding just what it is they are trying to keep from everybody else.

''In your case, from what you said to me in your letter, you are thinking about buying some ranch property. You should know the assets and any other information easily available about the seller, but also you look deeper. You just never know these days what might be hidden in somebody's closet. Lots of problems can arise in a hasty transaction. I could tell you stories that would make your hair stand on end!''

He took a strong swallow of cognac and his face

turned even redder. Again he reached up to pull at his too-tight collar, but this time the gesture was purely a reflex. The heat in the stuffy room and the effect of the brandy were clearly evident. Jonathan was very uncomfortable and trying not to show it. ''That the kind of investigation you want, Conrad?''

The familiarity grated on Conrad, but he said nothing.

''Yes,'' he replied. ''I plan on investing in more than Mr. Brunswick's ranch in Virginia City, but for now, yes. I would like you to go there yourself and very quietly look into this man's background. Anything you can tell me will help in my dealings with the man. Not that I suspect anything is wrong, but the man is too damned quiet for my taste. Could be I am just overly suspicious, but I don't want to spend money without knowing what I am buying, or why Hiram is selling. Reasons could change the price. Know what I mean?''

He wanted to find out everything he could about Hiram, but at the same time he felt a slight discomfort in telling this man all that he had. Conrad decided to be quiet and say no more than was absolutely necessary.

Jonathan stared straight into Conrad's eyes. He shook his head affirmatively and shifted his weight in the chair. His face was still flushed. He could feel the beads of sweat forming across his upper lip and at the back of his neck. His collar was too tight and it was becoming too much of an effort to keep his tie in place and straight. As he often did, he wondered why civilized men wore such uncivilized clothing. It was stifling in this room!

"Also," Conrad continued, "I need to know the usual things, the value of the land there and, since Brunswick is also one of the town's bankers, I can't very well ask him. Check sales, values, assessments, taxes, that kind of thing. I didn't want to use anybody from that area to do this investigating, so be very cautious about who you talk to. Virginia City is a very small town, and you know how they are in small towns. Don't use any of their local agents. Brunswick is too well known. And I just don't have the time to do all of this myself, especially right now. My daughter is being married soon".

"Well, congratulations, Conrad, so your daughter is getting married. Always good to get rid of one of the kids, especially girls, they can be a real expense, I hear. Never been married myself, never had the time."

Conrad winced at the unwanted familiarity. This was really a very unpleasant man.

"I realize you have other clients and will be busy learning all there is to know about your uncle's business, but could you give me an idea of just when you will have the time to go to Virginia City?" Conrad wanted to get this settled and be done with Jonathan.

Jonathan sat quietly for a moment. There was something about this cattleman that was interesting, an intensity—something different than anyone Jonathan had ever met. It was obvious he was a man of means; if nothing else, the clothes he wore indicated so. This gentleman had money. It showed in every move he made. But he was no fool. Only a fool would think so. Jonathan had to do this right. There could be a lot in this for him if he did this job just right. Jonathan was used to being in control when it came to investigating; before, as a bank examiner he had always had the upper hand. This was not the case with Conrad Fillmore. This was a very wary, intelligent man who was in complete control and used to that position. Jonathan would have to be careful.

"There's a lot of work for me at the office."

Conrad frowned and Jonathan continued. "But this is important to you, I can tell. I'm certain that the office is in good hands and will be when I am away. I will start just as soon as I can—it is just that I am taking over the company at a such an unfortunate time, but be assured I will assist you just as soon as it is possible for me to do so."

Conrad smiled.

"Now, about my fee."

Conrad knew that would be the next question, even before Jonathan had spoken it.

Chapter Four

Agatha stood by the front steps enjoying the coolness of the early evening. Everything had been ready for an hour. Clarisa was upset that the men were late. The dining room table was set with places for the three out-of-town visitors, along with Victor, Robert Graves, Comstock Mine's superintendent, and Bishop Patrick Manogue of St. Mary's Catholic Church.

The latter two were friends of the family who were always invited for any dinner parties when Hiram and Agatha entertained.

Hiram would sit at the head of the table, and Agatha, as the hostess, at the opposite end. A fine Burgundy wine would be served and the table set with a beautiful centerpiece of wildflowers to add color. Cigars and brandy were set up in the study for the men after dinner.

Agatha and Clarisa had prepared a fine meal. They were both accustomed to entertaining guests.

Brunswick Manor stood close to the peak of a mountain that rose sharply beyond a grove of cottonwoods. It overlooked the valleys and meadows that surround Virginia City. The veranda circled all four sides of the house, and the view was magnificent, especially tonight, or so it seemed to Agatha as she stood waiting for the guests to arrive. The air smelled clean with the scent of sage and the lilacs that bloomed close to the house. The evening sunset had turned the sky a brilliant coral, sending a soft glow over Agatha. She was completely unaware of just how beautiful she looked in her deep green satin gown, highlights glistening in her auburn hair, soft crimson on her cheeks.

The quiet was interrupted by the sound of horses coming up the canyon. By the time Agatha heard them through the clear evening air, they were coming through the front gate. The wagon with Nate was the first to arrive, then Hiram, Victor, and the bishop followed by four men, all on horseback. They circled around the manor toward the corral. Agatha lifted her hand in greeting, then walked to the side veranda that was closest to the barn and watched as the men tied up their mounts. She smiled as all six riders took off their hats, dusted themselves off, and almost in unison looked her way. Another special evening at Brunswick Manor had begun.

Dinner was going well. Bishop Manogue sat at Hiram's right with Robert Graves to his left. The rest sitting around the table included Ike Masterly who was at least six feet tall and skinny as a rail. His deeply tanned skin was the only indication that he was an outdoorsman. He was a very pleasant man. Conrad Fillmore sat next to Agatha, on her right. An unruly head of absolutely white hair was in contrast to a very ruddy face. He had, Agatha thought, the kind of complexion that would always give him trouble in the sun, unfortunate for a man who had chosen an outdoor life. To her left was Lucas Forester, quiet, ruggedly handsome with blond hair and very dark brown eyes. He seemed always, when looking her way, to find Agatha amusing. She found his glances exciting and irritating at the same time. It was very distracting. Victor entered little into the immediate conversation. His interest was, as usual, the food.

Agatha could tell that their guests were enjoying the evening. There was a good deal of hearty laughter, stimulating stories that were both interesting and fun, the food was delicious, and the wine perfect. Even Agatha felt a wonderful glow that just added to the feeling of expectancy she had been feeling all day.

"Nice place you have here." Conrad Fillmore was speaking. "Always wanted to see this place, heard a lot about it. And your daughter is even more beautiful than I had been led to believe, Hiram," he added.

Agatha blushed solidly.

Everyone seemed content to stay seated at the table, even Hiram, who was usually in a rush to finish and get on with business. He sat quietly listening to his guests and enjoying the attention that his beautiful daughter was receiving. Hiram disliked meeting new people but he found this evening pleasant and easy and was surprised himself.

Victor spoke. "You are all aware that Mr. Brunswick intends selling a large portion of his ranch. It will include everything but the house, the horse barn, and a small acreage. The rest, with cattle, is included. We are very busy at the bank these days and handling two businesses is getting to be a little too much. This is why he had me get in touch with all of you. While Hiram is of course my employer, I will be handling a good deal of the paperwork."

Hiram interrupted.

"What Victor says is quite true. Don't be afraid to discuss business in front of Bishop Manogue, Mr. Graves, or Victor. They are all close family friends."

The bishop rose.

"What say we retire to the study? If Miss Agatha will excuse us. There is some very good brandy waiting for us and I am so inclined. After that Bob and I both have other business to attend to this evening and will be leaving. You gentlemen can then talk away."

"Will you excuse us, Agatha?" It was Robert Graves who spoke.

The men retired to the study, but not before thanking their hostess and complimenting her on the delicious meal. Lucas Forester held back, and after the others had left the dining room stood quietly in front of Agatha. Only then did she realize how very tall he was. He had laugh lines around his eyes that showed pleas-

antly when he smiled. Again he had that amused
expression that puzzled her.

"We must do this again sometime." he smiled.

"You're welcome in our home anytime, Mr. Forester," she replied.

"That isn't exactly what I meant." He was smiling
that amused smile again.

Agatha blushed again. "We will have to talk about
that sometime soon."

Lucas Forester said not another word but gently lifted
her hand to his lips, lightly kissed her fingers, then
turned and walked into the study.

Much later, unable to sleep, Agatha stood at her
bedroom window and looked out at the night. Usually
guests in the house didn't disturb her, but tonight was
different—she had paced the floor, tried to read, tried
to sleep. She could hear the voices below, sudden
bursts of laughter and once, when someone walked
back to the kitchen, their boots' heavy tread retreating
and then returning. There was extra pie—that would
be Victor. Then she heard laughter in the hallway and
the sound of more boots as the men moved on out to
the veranda. She didn't understand her feelings or understand why she couldn't sleep or why she was now
watching the men as they rode out through the front
pasture and the ranch gates, one by one, except for the
last rider. Agatha knew immediately who it was by the
slow and deliberate way he walked. It was Lucas Forester; she remembered that easy walk. Still standing at
the bedroom window, she watched as Lucas stopped
his mount, a horse as dark as mahogany, and with quiet

deliberation lifted his hat from his head, looked up at Agatha silhouetted in her window, and as a gallant knight of old might have done, bowed with a flourish.

The recipient of his gesture stood rooted to the floor in delight and amazement.

The glowing feeling of expectancy that Agatha had felt all day now had meaning.

Morning had brought with it full sunshine. A few soft clouds moved across the sky. The hillsides were covered with pink, violet and yellow flowers.

A bustling noise from inside told Agatha that Nate and Clarisa were at it again. Voices could be heard coming from the kitchen. Agatha could hear Nate's infectious laugh.

"Get outa' my kitchen, you ornery cuss. You think I got nothin' to do but wait on you hand and foot! Just like a man, pain in the . . . " Clarisa's voice, her sentence unfinished, loudly exclaimed her usual fury.

But before she could say anything else there was another loud crash and Nate came flying through the door trying to balance a cup of hot coffee in one hand, and his hat in the other. His face was flushed and smiling.

"You two still arguing?" Agatha had to laugh.

Nate rushed off across the yard toward the bunkhouse. It was time to be busy. But behind him came a flushed and breathless Clarisa who stopped when she saw Agatha, put her hands on both hips, glanced sideways to see if anyone was watching, and then put her hands over her mouth to cover up her laughter.

"He is just too much, much too mighty much!"

With that Clarisa went back to the kitchen and Agatha was left alone standing on the veranda looking across the ranch. She was still thinking about the previous evening and what it could mean. Excitement and expectancy both held sway. There was no denying her own intense feelings, feelings she had never before experienced.

Hiram came out from the parlor, a massive pile of papers in his hands. He interrupted Agatha's thoughts.

"Did things go well last night, Father?" she asked as Hiram stretched his arms upward and yawned.

"Just fine. Of course they're still talking. I just don't know for certain who is the most interested, or if they will form any kind of partnership. Conrad Fillmore seems more inclined than the others. Asked a lot of questions. More than I thought were necessary, but then, Conrad has always been a cautious man.

"There's lots of room for someone to build a good house and the cow barn is adequate. Conrad's the one with the most to invest and he also has a family. The others, well, Ike's a widower and the others bachelors. At least that's the impression I got. I really feel good about it. We have more than we need, and once the deal is closed I can concentrate on the bank. We'll have the horses, maybe a few chickens. I think Clarisa would enjoy that. It's time I got out of the ranch business anyway."

"You aren't telling me everything, are you?" Agatha questioned. She knew her father all too well, and this was just not like him. He could easily handle the ranch and the bank, it had never been a problem before, it shouldn't be a problem now, not with all the help he had in both places.

"And don't give me that look! I know you too well. There's something wrong, isn't there? You wouldn't be this anxious and in such a hurry if there wasn't a problem. Now, out with it, what is wrong?"

Hiram looked at his daughter, then at the papers in his hand, and with a loud sigh sat down on the porch swing and began to move back and forth. He dropped the papers down on a side table and put his hands up to his face and rubbed his fingers through his beard. Taking his time, he began looking out through the trees and across the land that was his—his ranch, his life. Not until he had been sitting for some moments did he speak.

"Yes, something."

"Well, what? And don't scare me like this."

"It's nothing, really. You mustn't worry. I'm just tired, that's all. At my age a man has to begin to think about retirement. And besides, shouldn't you be thinking about other things, or people?"

"Have the others left town yet, or will they be coming here again?"

Her question hung in the air.

"Nice-looking man, that Mr. Forester, I thought you hadn't noticed." Hiram smiled.

"Father, what ever do you mean?" Agatha exclaimed with an exaggerated, artificial southern accent.

It felt good to have a moment of relaxed conversation with her father; he was usually so detached from everyday life and the ranch. Agatha had always handled things alone and had become accustomed to his quiet solitude. Even small moments of frivolity were welcome.

"So you did notice him. He certainly did notice you!"

"You didn't answer my question!" Agatha said.

"What question is that?"

"You know darned well what question." She laughed and then continued. "Are they coming back again? Clarisa and I need to know."

"No, I doubt it, they should be pulling out tomorrow morning."

Agatha tried not to show her disappointment.

Hiram stood and left the room quickly, heading for the library, and was gone before she could say anything else. Last evening had been so wonderful. Today was definitely not going to be as grand a day as yesterday.

Or so she thought.

She was wrong.

Evening came slowly as if the day was reluctant to end. A slight wind fluffed up the grassy meadows. The sky had turned a brilliant purple as the sun sank beneath the distant Sierra Nevada.

Agatha was drawn outside by the beauty of the evening with its cool breeze, deep blue sky, and the first evening star shimmering quietly in its own enormous world. She stood leaning on the porch post gazing upward, a shawl pulled tightly around her shoulders against the chill of early evening. All day she had been wrestling with her feelings. Why did she feel this way? What was it about this man who had just come into her life that was making her feel so disappointed in his leaving? What did she expect? Whatever it was, it was new, and it was pleasant. Agatha had always been happy with her life, or was she? She had the ranch and her father to look after, her volunteer work at the hospital, her friends, and her books. What was this new feeling that had intruded into her placid and happy life? With a heavy sigh she turned and headed for the door.

Before she could enter the house she heard what sounded like a wagon coming down the road. It turned into the ranch and headed directly to the side of the veranda where she stood with her hand still on the doorknob.

Agatha could not see who the lone driver was. A man, no doubt of that, no passengers, no supplies. All she could see was a wagon and a man she couldn't identify until he was close to the veranda. Then she could see that it was Lucas—there was no mistaking him for anybody else. The wagon came up the drive. He was returning to see her, and she was amazed at her feelings and emotions, which were so new and intense they were almost frightening.

"My God," she spoke out loud. "Have I fallen in love with this man?"

Lucas pulled the wagon up to the porch in front of Agatha. Stepping out, he glanced up at her and smiled. "Come on down here!" It was an order, but said in a deep, gentle voice.

Agatha did not move.

"Please."

Agatha walked slowly down the steps, never taking her eyes from his face. He took her hand and helped her up into the wagon, then got back on the other side and rode away down the path that led past the barn and pasture. Beyond the mountains the sunset gleamed like a brilliant bouquet, Agatha was certain she had never seen a more beautiful sight. Neither of them spoke as Lucas drove the team back across the fields to the highest point behind the ranch. Then he stopped.

"I have to leave tomorrow. We need to take a herd north, then I have to go to Kansas City. I've got a lot of unfinished business there, but it shouldn't take more than a month. Then I will be going on to San Francisco. My aunt Bea and I haven't had a good visit for years. She's not getting any younger and she hasn't been well. I really do have to see how things are with her. She raised me after my parents died, but it isn't just that I feel an obligation; she's a great lady. I guess you could say she's my best friend."

Lucas smiled and took her hand, squeezing it. "But before I left, I wanted to see you again."

"I wish you well, Lucas." It was all that Agatha could say. She found it difficult to speak to this man. She wanted to, but the words just would not come.

Lucas turned and looked directly into Agatha's eyes. He pushed a curl of hair gently back from her forehead. Agatha felt her breath quicken. He moved his gaze quietly over her face, then turned and drove the buggy back to the house.

He helped her down from the seat and, smiling,

walked her to the porch. "On my way back from Kansas City I'll be stopping in Virginia City. We need to talk again before I head for San Francisco. Will you be here?"

The question hung in the air.

"Of course. As I said before, you know you are welcome in our home anytime."

"And again, I will answer. That's not what I meant."

There was a look of intensity in his eyes as he suddenly grasped her shoulders and pulled her forward. His kiss was strong and intense.

With that Lucas went down the stairs and stepped back up into the wagon, then turned and looked up at Agatha, who stood on the veranda, her face scarlet, her eyes wide.

"I'm in love with you, Agatha Brunswick. I have never been more certain of anything in my life."

For a moment neither spoke. Agatha was too stunned to speak another word, and Lucas had said what he had come to say.

"Remember that and think about it until I get back."

Then, putting on his hat and taking up the reins, he rode away into the night.

Chapter Five—April 1875

Summer had come early to Kansas City. The humidity was unbearable. Heat seemed to rise in waves from the ground, and everyone moved in slow motion. People stayed indoors as much as possible. Children played in the city streets, splashing through the gutters filled with water that gushed unchecked from opened fire hydrants. Older people sat fanning themselves on front porches, lemonade stands did a great business, and those that could, slept at night on rooftops, but nothing helped when the humidity and heat were both this intense.

Jim Fitzgerald's Saloon was doing a tremendous business. The sign said, LADIES WELCOME IN OUR GENTEEL BACK ROOM. The bar was jammed elbow to elbow. The beer was cold, and even though the cold meat, cheese, and bread were free, not too many people were eating. It was too warm even for that.

At the far end of the bar a cowboy sat alone, his third mug of beer still full in front of him. Jim was used to barroom characters who wanted to be left alone, but in this case it was someone he knew. Usually the two of them had a great deal to talk and laugh about. Not so today. His friend Luke sat quietly, ignoring everybody including Jim. What was on Luke's mind Jim didn't know and didn't ask—not at first. Finally, when there was a lull in business, he walked to the other end of the bar to try and find out just what was bothering his friend.

"OK, partner, what's the trouble? You're too damned quiet, I'm thinkin'. Or is it none of my business?"

"You're right, Fitz, it isn't any of your business!" Lucas Forester replied. He was not smiling.

"OK, Bucko, if that's the way it is." Jim turned back to the other customers.

"Hey Jim!" Lucas leaned forward across the bar and grabbed Jim by the arm. Jim looked down at the hand holding him so firmly and glanced toward his friend, who loosened his grip.

"Come back here. I'm sorry," Lucas continued.

"Got a lot, and I do mean a lot, on my mind. And yes, I do need somebody to talk to."

"Hell, I've been doin' nothin' else for twenty-seven years."

* * *

The big-muscled Irishman picked up a towel from behind the bar and began polishing the already shiny bar.

"So what's botherin' you, pal o'mine?" The Irish brogue was unmistakable.

"You know Constance Fillmore, Conrad's daughter? Don't ask me how, but she seems to think we have an understanding. That's a lie, I do know how!"

Luke shook his head in disgust. Fitz could tell his friend was in a black mood.

"I just never let her know the truth, I don't love the woman, never have. It was one of those childhood things that grew from our being raised so close together. We're related, by marriage, oh heck, back there somewhere. I never asked her to marry me, it's just that we have been friends since way before my Aunt Bea moved to San Francisco. Being raised together, Connie just took it for granted, and me being the dumb ox that I am, I never dreamed she was serious. I've been too busy to give it much thought—that is, until now. The whole idea has always seemed too ridiculous to even imagine taking seriously. But she has, Constance has!"

Fitz ran his fingers through his untamed red hair, then put down the bar rag, crossed his arms over his enormous chest, tilted his head to one side, stared at his friend, and frowned. He picked up the cloth again, lifted Luke's glass, and wiped the damp circular ring clean. He looked down into the half-filled glass of beer now flat and warm, tossed its contents into the sink, and filled it to the brim with a cold brew. Only then did he speak.

"Hey, Fitz, I wanna a beer!" A customer from the other end of the bar was voicing his objection to the two men in conversation.

"In a minute, in a minute, hold your horses. You still got half a mug, fella!" Fitz replied.

"Go on, so what's happening, she finally trying to tie the knot?"

"Not just that. Conrad and I just finished a trip out west. We had business in Virginia City, and while there I met the one woman in the world for me. Lord but it sounds stupid! I fell in love with her the moment I looked into those beautiful eyes.

"Then what do I find when I get back? What do I face? Connie has told her father, every friend she has in the world, and would you believe it, the minister, that we are getting married! I was afraid that this was going to happen. All the way to Virginia City I kept thinking about something her mother had said to me. I couldn't be sure, but I should have been. The signs were all there. Talk about putting my head in the sand. I just kept putting off doing anything about the problem. And if I were honest with myself, I should have guessed what was happening here!"

"Well, pal, why didn't you tell the lady before you left when you had those suspicions. It's not like you to put off something important. There isn't any sense in waiting," Fitz said in his straightforward manner.

"Hold it a minute, Lucas, my friend!"

Jim went to the far end of the bar to take care of his

other thirsty customers. Finally he had time again for his friend.

"OK, what else?"

"Fitz, I heard it from people, a lot of people. I came in here to calm down. Even so, it is going to be difficult. Her family is expecting it, so is my Aunt Bea, although I don't think Bea ever really liked Connie that much. This isn't going to be easy! Guess I came in here to get the courage to go and settle this thing with Connie."

"Luke, I never knew you to be afraid of anything!"

"But a woman scorned, or so she will think, that's something else, Fitz! I'd rather wrestle a bear!"

"Ha! You might be when her dad gets the news. Does he know this other gal, what's her name?"

"Agatha! Fitz, the most beautiful, warm, strong woman you ever met. Hazel eyes, beautiful hair, tall— darn it, man, I love that woman so much I can't sleep nights thinking about her. I have got to get back to Virginia City before somebody else gets smart and marries her."

"Ain't no time like the present. Better go face the music and get this misunderstanding settled."

"True, I just never thought much about it. When we were kids my brother Thomas and I always gave in to her, Connie being the only girl, usually. We'd sneak off alone whenever we could, but somebody would always pull us back and make us play with poor little Connie. Maybe that's why I let this thing go on for so long. When Tom died, well, that just made it worse. Maybe you're right. It won't make it any easier to sit here and talk."

"Better get crackin'. Or else you'll find yourself married to Constance Fillmore, and wondering how it happened!"

The dressmaker had perspiration running down her arms and inside the back of her dress. It made the material cling to her body and the heat seem even worse. She kept wondering why people wanted to marry in June, why not December when it was cold, or September? Here it was the first week in April and hotter than blazes.

"Stand still, dear. I know it's hot, but we have to get this hem just right."

"I can't stand still! This darned lace is scratching me everywhere! Can't you hurry! I've been standing here for hours, and Lucas will be getting to the house soon, I want to be there to meet him. I know he'll be anxious to see the dress."

"Constance, dear, the groom never sees the dress before the wedding, you know that! And young ladies do not swear!"

Emily Fillmore was sitting on a horsehair chair and wiping the perspiration from her face. A big woman with ample bosom and hair piled in a huge knot at the top of her head, she found the warm sewing room insufferable, but it had to be borne if Connie's dress was going to be ready for a June wedding.

"Darn you, that last pin stuck me! Can't you be more careful?"

"Constance!" her mother exclaimed. "Young ladies don't swear. I told you that before! What ever will Mrs. Stokes think!''

"It's all right, Mrs. Fillmore. I understand. It's this awful heat, it's bothering everybody. Anyway, I'll be finished in a minute. There, that's the last pin. Now stand very still while I pull the dress off over your head.''

The dressmaker spoke in a mumble with a bunch of straight pins sticking out of her mouth.

Constance stood, golden hair circling her face, her pert little nose wrinkled in distaste as the dressmaker lifted the dress up over her head. Then she sighed. "Thank goodness that's over! Let me get back in my cotton and out of here!''

Later, in the carriage, Mrs. Fillmore spoke again to her daughter. "You don't think you are rushing things a little, dear, do you? After all, you haven't even talked to Lucas yet about a date for the wedding. June second isn't that far away, there are so many things to do. And Lucas may have business plans—he is always so busy in the summer. Don't you think you should be waiting a little longer, this telling friends, and all? I don't think you were wise.''

"Oh, Mother, you know men; if I wait until he's settled we'll never get a date set. Just leave him to me. I can handle Lucas.''

The carriage continued down the hot street. No air was moving. It was difficult to breathe, the humidity heavy and moist. But Constance Fillmore sat serene and placid, certain that her marriage plans would turn out just fine.

At the other end of town Lucas was leaving Fitz's bar. He would have something to say about wedding plans. Yes, there would be a wedding if he had his say, but not a wedding that included Constance.

Lizbeth was teasing Agatha who, while Lizbeth kept talking about the children, church, and other activities in town, was oblivious to anything she was saying.

"And so I decided to become an atheist. I don't believe in God anymore. What do you think about that, dear?"

"That's nice," Agatha answered.

"Agatha Brunswick, you haven't heard a word I've been saying. Where in the world are you? You certainly aren't here! Now, you tell me this minute, this very minute, what is going on in that pretty brain of yours. It's one of those men that came to dinner. I knew it, I just knew it, I just told Frank this morning that I knew something was going on with you and one of those cattlemen." She continued to rattle on.

"Hold it a minute!"

Agatha was laughing and trying, as she always did, to get Lizbeth to slow down just long enough to get a word in edgewise. It was never easy.

And she did have something to say. Something important.

The sun had dropped behind the bare hills around Virginia City and a sweet softness had come to the valley that surrounded Brunswick Manor. Agatha was deep in thought looking out across the ranch, as she usually did after supper. The day's work was done and the noisy day had settled into quiet evening. She was alone with her thoughts except for a cowhand who stood in deep shadow at the side of the bunkhouse. She watched as he lifted a small sack of tobacco from his shirt pocket, pulled it open, and became busy with the work of making a cigarette. He too looked unready for sleep.

Only a week had passed since Lucas had left for the east. Agatha wondered if it had all been in her imagination. Had he really said he loved her? She clung to the memory, could not turn away from her feelings, could not think of anything else. She would rationalize that it was ridiculous to think anything would come of this so new relationship, even if he had declared his love. But try as she might, she could not stop thinking about this man who had entered her life so swiftly and left a mark on her heart that could not be erased.

He had sent her a card upon his arrival in Kansas City. She had read the words in eager anticipation.

All it had said was, "Remember yesterday and think about tomorrow!" It was signed simply "Luke." Obviously the last was a nickname; she liked the sound of that one word.

Her friend Lizbeth Roberts was expecting again. She already had four other little ones at home to look after and a husband that was busy in the mines most of the time. Agatha tried to go down to visit Lizbeth and her children at least twice a week to take some of the enormous burden off her friend's shoulders. When not at Lizbeth's, she looked for books to read and add to her library; Tuesday afternoons were set aside for the ladies' auxiliary at the Presbyterian church, and Mondays and Fridays for the hospital.

Nate was driving her down to visit Lizbeth one early morning, and as they passed the parsonage the scent of honeysuckle and roses filled the air. Agatha looked around her at the tiny Victorian houses that sat along C Street and wondered where Lucas was at that moment, and if it was as beautiful as here in Virginia City.

Kansas City was being deluged with water. It was raining in sheets that caused the horses to shy at every turn. The roads had turned to quagmires of mud, and people had to slosh down the streets through what had been created by a sudden spring storm. It was a relief of sorts after all of the heat, but the storm was so intense that it was creating havoc everywhere. The rain was splashing ankle deep. Lucas could not find a hansom, and was in no mood to walk the entire distance to visit Constance and settle things. He would have to take his horse and suffer in the rain. There was no other way.

Constance was crying. Her mother was fuming. Her father was enjoying a tall whiskey and soda and ignoring the two women, who always seemed to dominate everything with their presence. It was easier to just have a drink, smoke a cigar, read his paper, and plan on his next trip out of town away from this house that was no longer a home. He wondered if it had ever really been one. And if not, whose fault was it?— probably his own. He had never had the gumption to set his foot down, or maybe he just didn't care any-more. It really didn't matter. Connie was happy, or so she seemed, and he did dote on his beautiful daughter, who was their only child.

"Why hasn't he been here? Darn the man. It's been three days, three days, and he hasn't been near this house! Everybody else has seem him but me! It is embarrassing! It is inexcusable! What possible reason could he have to stay away! I won't get in touch with him, I won't! You hear me? I won't!"

The whole room vibrated with the sound of Connie's screaming.

"Dear, remember what I said, ladies do not swear! And besides, he'll be here, you just wait. He will be walking up to the door any minute."

"In this rain! I just bet he will!"

She screamed even louder. The tears were gone, her face was flushed scarlet, her blond curls dancing around her face, and her tiny turned-up nose had become even redder than her face.

Just then, as if on cue, the knocker sounded. No one moved.

"Answer the door, Josephine, answer the darned door!" Constance was still swearing.

Conrad glanced up over the top of the paper, flipped some ash from his cigar, took a sip from his drink, and then lifted the paper back up to cover his face. He continued reading.

Josephine finally appeared, rushing in from the kitchen while wiping her hands on her apron. She turned and gave Constance a withering look. She had obviously been in the middle of something that required her attention for dinner.

At last she opened the door. There stood Lucas Forester, his face frowning, his clothes soaking wet and his boots muddy. It really wasn't the right time for Constance to be in ill temper. But she was about to find that out.

"Lucas, darling!" The tears were gone, the fury ended. "Where have you been? Oh, sweetheart, you're soaked to the skin. Here, let me take your coat."

"Never mind, I won't be here long," Lucas said as he tried to wipe his wet face with a handkerchief that was as wet as he was. It did little good.

"Don't be ridiculous," Conrad said. The newspaper was now a forgotten pile on the floor. "You're staying for dinner, of course."

"I can't. I just came to speak to Connie alone, if you two will excuse us."

With that he took her by the wrist and marched out into the foyer, then into the library, shutting the door behind them.

Emily smiled up at Conrad.

"I told you, he's going to propose properly, and everything will be just fine."

"Suré, sure!" Conrad replied. He had picked up his paper and was again too busy to hear what his wife said.

Inside the library Constance had thrown her arms around Lucas's neck and was kissing him soundly on the mouth. Lucas in turn was trying to disengage her tangling arms.

"Oh my, but you are wet." She removed her arms and looked longingly up into his eyes. A drop of rain-water was dripping from her nose. She brushed it away with a quick motion of her hand.

"We have to settle something, Connie. Sit down."

"Lucas, you look angry, what ever is the matter?"

"I told you to sit down! Now sit down!"

Connie did as she was told. She sat down, folded her hands together in her lap, and looked up at Lucas while fluttering her eyelids. She smiled demurely.

"You know darned well what's the matter. You've told everybody in town we are going to be married. You also know I never asked you to be my bride and that I have no intention of marrying you. Not next month, next year, not ever!"

Constance sat staring wide eyed at him, her mouth open, her face beginning to turn red again. The demure smile was gone.

"I'm sorry, Connie," he continued, finally quieting down after the terrible ride through the storm. "I don't mean to hurt you, but you know I'm telling you the truth. There isn't anything between us, there never has been. Whatever you imagined was childhood nonsense, the kind of thing that grown people put away, like their toys, as they grow up. Connie, now it's your turn to grow up. You aren't going to marry your imagined boyhood sweetheart."

She still sat and stared. The tears were coming now. It wasn't just losing Lucas that was making her angry, but at the embarrassment she would feel in front of her friends.

"Don't pull that on me, Constance Fillmore, I have seen that little trick too many times. Now you march outside and tell your parents the truth. This charade has ended!"

With that, he pulled her from the chair, again by the wrist, and marched her back to the parlor to confront her parents.

The two of them entered the room, Constance being almost dragged into her parents' presence.

"Tell them, Connie. You started this mess, you finish it."

"Daddy, Lucas refuses to keep his commitment. He won't marry me."

The tears were again cascading down her red cheeks. She ran and threw herself into her father's arms. Conrad, surprised by this sudden emotional charge, stood looking first at his wife, then at Lucas, and finally at his daughter, now clinging to his body.

"Oh Daddy!" she wailed. "What can I do, what can I tell my friends?" The tears continued.

"You can tell them any thing you want. What the heck is going on, Lucas? I thought this was all settled?"

"I'm sorry, Conrad, I never asked your daughter to marry me. It's a misunderstanding. But I will not ruin my life—and not incidentally Connie's—with a marriage that would be a disaster."

"I think you'd better leave, Lucas." It was Emily who spoke.

"I'm sorry, Emily. The last thing I would ever do was hurt any of you. You know how close we have always been. But I cannot do what I cannot do! Not to save face, not for Connie, or for you, or Conrad. You can tell people whatever you like. I will be glad to be the villain in this. Just let me know what to say, and I will say it.''

With that Lucas Forester left the company of Conrad, his wife, and his daughter and headed for the door.

''Just a minute, Luke!'' Conrad said indignantly. ''You can't just walk in and make that kind of announcement. It's that girl in Virginia City, isn't it?''

Luke stood for a moment with his back to the room and then turned. ''No Conrad, it isn't. Yes, I am in love with Agatha. The minute I looked at her my life changed. It won't ever be the same again. But that has absolutely nothing to do with this. Connie made up her mind that she wanted something she couldn't have. It's always been that way. She's spoiled rotten; you know that and I know that. But this time she cannot have it her way. I don't love her, I never have, and I most certainly never proposed.''

He took a few more steps into the hallway, turned back and spoke again. ''I'm sorry, Connie, really I am. You too, Conrad and Emily. We've been friends, close friends for too long to let anything like this misunderstanding change things. Make me the heavy, or better yet have Connie tell everyone she changed her mind. But a marriage in this house is just not going to include me. That's final.''

''Darn you, Lucas Forester!''

Connie's face was purple with rage, her shoulders stiffened, and her body arched. She grabbed a vase from the mantelpiece and threw it full force at Luke, who ducked just in time. It smashed heavily against the wall. Screaming, she rushed at him and started beating him on the chest.

"I won't have this! How dare you, you skunk, you lying skunk. I'll pay you back if it's the last thing I ever do!"

Luke grabbed her wrists and pushed her back into the room, then he dislodged himself and walked out into the hall, opened the front door, and slammed it behind him.

Conrad was not a real family man, but when it came to his honor or the honor of anyone with his name, especially Connie, that was another thing entirely. Lucas Forester was not going to get away with this. Not for one minute. So Lucas Forester was in love with Agatha Brunswick, eh! Conrad would take care of those two. He would find a way, some way, any way. There must be something. There was Jonathan Woodrow. Let's just see what he would dig up. It might take some time, but things were already in motion. What had started out as a simple checkup on a business associate had now become a vendetta.

"Connie, be quiet and sit down!" Emily spoke in a voice that left Constance no choice. She sat down and watched as Conrad paced the floor.

"Don't you worry, I'll take care of that good-for-nothing. In the meantime tell your friends you've changed your mind, Constance. There isn't anything else you can do. And I think a trip to Europe is in order. A trip abroad would do you a world of good."

A few days later Lucas Forester left for Virginia

City, Constance and Emily Fillmore for New York City and a trip to England, and Jonathan Woodrow for Philadelphia.

And Agatha Brunswick waited.

Chapter Six

For a man of action, Lucas found the trip back to Virginia City too long and very boring. He tried not to be impatient, but the need to see Agatha again was all that seemed important. The scenery seemed to be floating by the window—Lucas found it completely uninteresting. His riding companion was a heavy woman who seemed to be all elbows as she kept digging down into her valise. In desperation he went to the back of the train where a group of men were playing cards and where it was possible to get a glass of port. The friendly bartender he had seen on his previous trip was not in attendance and Lucas was disappointed. It would have been pleasant to talk again to the tall black man who had been so tolerant and understanding.

It also seemed somewhat cooler in the club car, and it definitely was more comfortable than in his seat next to the woman with the elbows. He watched a card game for a time and had several glasses of wine, which relaxed him enough to get some much-needed sleep. He gradually realized just how tense he had been. The effects of the scene with Connie had taken their toll.

He arrived in Carson City too late to catch the train to Virginia City. Although anxious to see Agatha, he did need some rest and a chance to wash away the dust of the long journey. He was smiling in spite of being so tired, and he was also aware just how much like a young schoolboy he felt at the thought of seeing her again. He wanted to be at his best.

Lucas checked into the Ormsby House, had something to eat, washed, and was asleep in a comfortable bed the minute his head rested on the pillow.

In the morning Lucas found his way back to the station and boarded the Virginia & Truckee for the now familiar ride through Gold City.

As the train pulled into the station he was surprised to see Nate standing there, hat in hand and a frown on his face. Jumping down onto the platform, he rushed to the cowboy, afraid that something was wrong with Agatha.

''Nate, something's wrong! Tell me it isn't Agatha!''

''No, but we got this here telegram at the ranch. It's for you. Come from San Francisco. Nobody opened it, but a telegram, well, it has to be important. We knew you were coming—Miss Agatha has been waiting. She got your letter.'' He smiled.

Lucas opened the message. It read:

"Your Aunt very ill. Come at once. Sending telegram Kansas City to be certain you get news." It was signed by Bea's lawyer.

"It's my Aunt Bea, Nate. She's very ill. I won't have much time here, but I must see Agatha right away."

The ride through town and up the mountain took a very short time, but Lucas thought it took forever. All he could think of was Agatha, lovely Agatha!

The surrey went through the front gates slowly, and there on the veranda, just as he had dreamed she would be, stood Agatha. His heart seemed to turn over inside his chest, she was so beautiful. Nate pulled up in front of the house and Lucas stepped down from the surrey. Nate continued on toward the barn. He doubted either of them noticed that he was gone.

Lucas and Agatha stood just a short distance apart. Neither spoke at first.

"You're here." Her voice was low and warm.

Lucas walked up the few steps and stood in front of his love. Tiny strands of her hair were softly moving about her face as a light breeze stirred the air. Taking her hand, he led her back through the kitchen. Clarisa was nowhere to be seen. They walked together into the parlor and Lucas shut the sliding doors. They were alone. Agatha dropped his hand and moved toward the fireplace, her back to him. Walking up behind her, he put his hand on her shoulder and turned her around slowly. With his left hand he brushed back the wayward curls, and with his right arm pulled her toward him, looked into her eyes, and kissed her fully on the lips.

He held her tightly in his arms for a full minute. Only then did he speak.

"You waited."

"Yes!" she answered, breathless, her heart pounding with such strength Agatha found it difficult to speak.

"I love you, more than you can know."

"I know, I feel the same. If you hadn't come back, I don't know what I would have done." She had finally found her voice.

"Come over to the divan. I wanted to just sit for a while and look at you, but there isn't much time. We do have to talk."

Agatha reached up and touched his cheek. He caught her fingers in his hand and leaned forward to kiss her again.

"God, how I love you!" he exclaimed.

"I can't stay, Agatha. The telegram Nate brought me was from Bea's lawyer. She's much worse. I have to go to San Francisco right away."

"Oh, Lucas, I'm so sorry. Of course you must go. I'll be here when you get back—waiting," she added.

"We're going to be married. You know that, don't you?"

"Are we?" she asked, smiling.

He lifted her to her feet. "Don't you dare tease me, don't you dare!"

Laughing, she hugged him around the waist and put her head on his shoulder, his warm, strong shoulder. It felt more wonderful than anything else in the world, natural, comfortable. Right here in his arms was where she belonged.

"I know you have to go, but I shall miss you so very much. Tell your aunt I send my best wishes for a speedy recovery. We haven't met, but I know I will love her too."

"Nate will take me right back to the station. As soon as I can I'll write. I'm terrible at letters, but I'll write, I promise! In any case, I shouldn't be more than a few weeks. If I'm going to be longer, I'll get in touch somehow. And then I am coming back. In the meantime you can keep busy arranging a wedding. Your wedding and mine! Lord, but that sounds good!"

Less than an hour later Lucas turned around in the front seat of the surrey as Nate took him back into town and the start of his journey to San Francisco. He saw Agatha standing in the sunlight, one hand shielding her eyes, the other waving good-bye.

Conrad Fillmore was glad to see the ship pulling away out of New York Harbor. He sighed in relief. Constance was crying as he watched from the wharf; Emily stood fussing over the collar of her coat and seemed not to notice that they were on their way. At the last moment she looked up and sent him a short wave.

He didn't think Jonathan Woodrow had had time to get to Virginia City, but in any case he was going to keep after him about the investigation. Maybe Lucas Forester thought he could hurt Connie and get away with it, but Conrad knew better. He certainly wasn't going to let any past friendship get in the way of re-taliation. There was nothing he could think of in Luke's past that could sour the relation between Lucas and the Brunswick girl. But there had to be something; nobody was perfect. He was determined to destroy any happiness Lucas looked forward to.

The end of the evening found Conrad, content after a fine dinner, ready to sleep. Tomorrow he could concentrate on his plan to return the hurt to Lucas that he had heaped on Connie!

Nurses were scurrying around doing their morning rounds. Bea Forester woke to the noise of a door opening. Her medication had worn away and the pain of her illness seemed to slam into her body like a hammer. She moaned aloud.

"Morning, Miss Bea, how are we feeling this morning?"

"*We* are feeling like a pile of manure, we are!" She emphasized the "we"!

"Well this hot tea and toast should fix everything!"

"The heck you say!" Bea replied. Her voice was weak and thin, but filled with determination.

"Where is the darned doctor!"

"Now, now, Miss Bea. Dr. Hastings will be here in a minute. He's just down the hall." She fluffed up Bea's pillow and tried straightening up the bed.

"Cut that out! Why bother, they'll be in any minute to change the sheets. It hurts when you move this bed of pain. Get out of here! Get out!"

The nurse frowned a little and started toward the door.

"Come back here, Martha."

The chubby nurse turned around.

"I'm sorry. I really am. I hate waking up, it just hurts so much." Bea was close to tears. "To be so helpless, darn it! I wish Lucas would get here."

Martha moved back to the bed and took Bea's hand.

"I know, dear, I really do. Dr. Hastings will give you something for the pain. They've tried to find Lucas, and they will, they really will.

"Your nephew means a lot to you, doesn't he?"

Bea closed her eyes and again shuddered with the pain that racked her body.

"You just wait a minute, honey, I'll get you something." Martha left the room.

Bea squeezed her eyes shut, as if in doing so the pain would disappear. It did not. She tried to push herself up higher on the pillow but the thing kept sliding farther down her back and she was cursing to herself as the door opened. Martha had returned with a small glass of water. She put out her hand.

"Here, hon, you swallow these now. You'll feel better. Now don't you worry."

Bea swallowed the pills and lay back on the pillows again. Her face was white and beads of sweat were breaking out on her forehead. If only Lucas would get here so she could just die. It hurt so very much.

Hiram could feel the warmth of the Nevada sun on his shoulders. It didn't seem to help the pain that pulsated through his chest and down his left arm. He moaned aloud.

"Darn it, darn it!"

With his left hand he clumsily pulled open the desk drawer and extracted a small white box, fumbled with the clasp and finally got it open. He placed one pill under his tongue, closed the box, and replaced it where he had found it, clear at the back behind a stack of papers. It wouldn't do for any of the help to know that he was on medication. Especially not until his cattle deal was over and done with. Only he and his doctor knew of his condition. Not even Agatha was to know, not yet.

Agatha had ridden Jubilee to the far pasture high above town. For the first time she noticed the immensity of the sky, today such a deep blue that it seemed to shrink all of the earth below into miniature. She thought about all the wonderful people in her life, her father, friends, and now Lucas, who was at that moment on a train headed for San Francisco. She heard the mournful sound of the train whistle as it was rounding the bend going toward Gold City.

"What a lonely sound that is." Only Jubilee was there to hear her words. Not until she knew the train was really on its way did she turn and ride Jubilee slowly back down to the barn. She wondered just how long it would be before she would see Lucas again.

The hospital corridor was quiet. Only the sound of a nurse, her thick-soled shoes making muffled footstep noises in another part of the wing, proved that not everyone was asleep.

Lucas found Room 104 and slowly pushed the door open. A soft light shone through the window. Aunt Bea lay, eyes closed, in shadow. He stood for a moment just looking her way.

"Don't just stand there, boy, get over here!" Her usually vibrant voice was a tiny echo of its former self, her body a gentle silhouette.

Luke moved to her side and picked up her hand, the skin thin as a whisper, the bones visible, the strength gone. He wanted to cry.

"How are you Aunt Bea?"

"Dying, darn it all!" She opened her eyes. "I had a dream last night. You got married to a beautiful lady. It was funny, I was in the room, way off to one side and nobody would talk to me. They all acted like I wasn't there. It was infuriating! Seems they couldn't see me at all. Then you turned around and looked straight at me and smiled. And you said something like, this is all right, isn't it, Aunt Bea? What do you make of that Lucas? Some crazy dream."

"Not so crazy. She's already said yes."

"It isn't Connie, is it, hon?"

"No," he answered.

"Good. Never did like that brat!"

"I had a feeling you didn't. But Bea, don't blame Connie, it isn't all her fault. She was simply spoiled all of her life. Down deep she is a nice person and I expect one day she will find the right man. It just isn't me!"

"Tell me about her, Lucas."

"Who?" Lucas asked.

"Don't play with me, boy! Who is this new woman? And she'd better be special!"

Lucas was quiet for a while, just smiling.

"You look like the Cheshire Cat—now on with it!"

"Her name is Agatha. She lives in Virginia City. I knew I was in love, really in love, for the first and only time. Never thought it would be that way with me, which is probably why I have not married before. There just hasn't been anybody else. But Agatha—oh, Bea, she is so beautiful, so good, so perfect. Lord, I sound like a man in love, don't I, Bea?"

Bea made a sound deep in her throat, her head moved to one side and her hand went completely limp in Lucas's.

"Bea, Aunt Bea?"

No answer came. He shook her shoulders tenderly, but there was no response. He ran out through the door and shouted for a nurse.

Later, as Lucas sat holding Bea's tired hand, she slipped quietly away.

The early morning sun was gently pushing away the darkness of the night.

"She was waiting for you, sir. It was obvious to us all that she stayed alive just long enough to see you. She loved you very much, Mr. Forester. We did everything we could to ease the pain. I hope you can find some comfort in that."

Lucas stood looking out across the bay. One beautiful woman had come into his life, another had left it.

There was so much to do here now, but so much happiness ahead of him with Agatha. If only he had been able to tell Bea all about what had happened in Virginia City. It was too late for the words to be spoken but somehow he knew that Bea would approve and want him to move on with his life. She had been that kind of woman. She had taught him well.

Lucas turned and left the hospital. The sun was now high in the morning sky.

The funeral was over. It had been quiet, private, and done exactly as Bea had wished. Her butler had supplied Lucas with all the necessary details and her lawyer had started probate. There was little left to do.

In Bea's beautiful house near the top of Knob Hill, Lucas stood looking back into the parlor from the foyer. It was on this exact same spot, so many years ago, that he had seen this house for the first time when Bea brought him here to visit. He had been a frightened little boy then. It was before his parents had died, and his first journey away from home. Later he would call it home.

The rooms were naked and void of furnishings. He could not remember a time in his life that he had felt so alone. There hadn't even been time to get in touch with Agatha since his arrival in San Francisco.

He couldn't bring himself to walk out the door, and started moving again from room to room and then up the wide staircase and into the tiny garret room that had been his as a boy. It seemed eons ago that he had pretended that this was the officers' deck of a sailing ship and he the captain.

He moved on into the upstairs sitting room. The fireplace was cold and empty now, the windows staring out across the bay. A freighter was moving through a heavy fog bank that was slowly drifting up toward the steep and twisted streets. Soon the world would be cushioned with its silence.

"How many times have we sat here together, Aunt Bea?" Lucas asked the empty room.

And now the realization really came to him—Bea was gone. He had been too busy before today to let grief move into his heart and mind. It was all over. But he did not have an empty heart. He had Agatha to return to.

Fog rolled up the hills in huge puffs, covering everything on its way, leaving the tips of chimneys and tops of buildings suspended as if they were floating in the air. And as it came up the last hill toward the empty house, even the sounds of the city were gone. Lucas stood alone in the empty room, feeling as if the whole world had stopped moving.

As he was staring out across the mist something moved, and for a moment the street scene came back into focus. A young woman, her shawl pulled tightly around her shoulders, stopped, looked up and down the street, and hurried across, then melted into the fog.

Lucas had to leave; he moved through the empty room, went down the stairs and walked out the front door. He slammed it shut and walked down the steep, winding street. His footsteps left no echo anywhere.

The fog was thick as cotton. Everything around him had disappeared; the houses were undefined, the streets vague shadows. He looked back toward the house on Knob Hill. It too had disappeared. He did not look back again.

Lucas Forester was going back to Virginia City, to Brunswick Manor, to a new life, to Agatha.

Jason McBride was a Scotsman who loved his whisky. It didn't seem to affect his job at the Wilson & Anderson Brewery, and his bosses liked him. He would often come to work a little under the weather, but Jason kept on working, loading kegs on the long flatbed wagon. Simon, the loading boss, said there was no finer man on the San Francisco docks than Jason McBride—strong as a bull and just as stubborn. How the man could work that hard and then keep on half the night was a wonder; he was an absolute marvel.

Most of the time they would keep him on the docks, but every now and again they would need a driver, and Jason would fill in. He was a much better dock hand than a driver. A man had to know how to handle a team to get through some of the narrow streets and up and down the hills.

Jason was feeling poorly, poorly indeed, but he kept on working and telling jokes to the other workers, keeping to himself that he felt just as bad as a man could who had tried to win a Scotch whisky–drinking contest at Gregory's—and lost, at that. He got out of his bed this morning and couldn't remember a thing about how he had gotten into it!

"God almighty, how I need a drink!" he said out loud and moaned. His buddy Nick looked his way and smiled. Nick knew him better than anyone and was certain Jason had a beauty of a hangover today. They were very busy at the brewery and Jason McBride was not in the mood for any of it, especially when he knew he would be doing the delivering.

The wagon was just about ready to go and the fog just kept rolling in. It was going to be a rotten trip. Better go and have a drink before he left.

"Get this thing outa here!" the foreman roared.

"Just a second. Keep your shirt on. Gotta go and get my coat." Jason moved off into the dark innards of the warehouse.

Feeling around the wall, he found the peg that held his mackinaw and pulled the coat down. He yanked a bottle out of the pocket, opened it, took a healthy swig and then, for good measure, he took a second.

Now that was more like it. He smiled.

Jason pulled the team away from the dock and started out. The fog was heavier on Montgomery Street and he cursed to himself. "Darn the luck!"

Dropping one hand from the reins, he reached again for his bottle. Hell, he thought, nobody can see me in this stuff.

From somewhere out of a side street came another wagon that passed just in front of the team, and they shied. It was all Jason could do to keep them steady, but not steady enough, for at that moment a dog started chasing the wagon and barking. The vehicle went wild.

The reins gone, Jason hung on for dear life, his eyes

wide and wild. Suddenly, there was a terrifying jolt, and somebody screamed. The wagon went weaving down the road, its horses uncontrolled.

It was the last thing Jason could remember as he was flung backward into the wagon bed.

And it was the last thing Lucas Forester would remember for a very long time.

As people started to gather at the scene, a letter addressed to Agatha Brunswick, Brunswick Manor, Virginia City, Nevada, slipped unnoticed into water running down the gutter. It floated, soggy and dirty, its inky address obliterated, into an opening to the sewer line beneath the street, and was gone.

The skies above the mountains were heavy. Agatha was riding her mare on the hill behind the mansion. It was time to get back, it looked as if it might rain. A herd of wild horses came thundering past, and Jubilee shied. Agatha pulled back on the reins and held the horse still until they were gone.

A flash of lightning lit up the sky, and the far-off sound of thunder vibrated across the valley. The horse shied again as the wind picked up and a cool blast buffeted the air. It wasn't like Jubilee to be this nervous; Agatha wondered what could be wrong with her.

Agatha pulled her coat tightly around her body and shivered, violently.

"It's not that cold! Why am I suddenly so cold?"

Chapter Seven—July 1875

Mildred Rainey was humming, arms up to her elbows that were covered with flour, her strong legs and huge body moving back and forth as she kneaded bread dough. A long strand of gray hair kept falling down over her eyes and she would push it away with a floured hand, never losing a stroke on the breadboard. Lucas was fascinated watching her.

"How in the world do you do it?" he asked.

"Do what?"

"Manage to keep this house so nice, cook like a Paris chef and bake, well, look at me! I've put on weight like crazy!"

"The doctors said you needed fattening up. This is the place to do it. Your Aunt Bea would want me to take care of you." She smiled for a moment, forgetting the work she was doing.

"You cannot imagine how much I miss her."

Lucas sat quietly sipping his coffee. He felt good. Except for the bandage that circled his head and a slight limp, there was no way to tell how life threatening his injuries had been. To him they were maddening. The outside pain could be healed, but the realization that he could remember nothing of who he was or anything about his life before the accident was tormenting. Only the fact that Bea's old friend Mildred worked as a volunteer at the hospital had brought the two of them together. Her help now was immeasurable. But the hospital records were not enough to tell him anything else. All that he had found of his past was an empty house that stared out across the bay. When he had finally been able to go there he found it as lonely and empty as he felt.

"You remembering something, Luke?"

"Flashes, Mildred. They come and go, but nothing I can seem to grab hold of and keep. It's driving me crazy." He reached up, grabbing at the air, then clenching his hands into tight, empty fists.

"The doctors say it will take time, you have to be patient. It can't be easy. You need to smile, though, at least once in a while. You've got me, remember?"

Her ruddy, warm face crinkled up into a fat smile that made her green eyes twinkle. Lucas loved this sweet angel of a lady who had helped bring him back from death.

Somewhere in his past there were people—friends, people he worked with. There had to be. There wasn't any family, Mildred had told him that. But what did he do, where did he live? All she knew was what Bea had told her. He lived in Missouri somewhere, or did, and raised cattle and was single. Mildred wasn't even sure of these facts. Luke's mind would go over and over these same thoughts until his head would pound with recurring headaches and, until he was a lot better, there was no way for him to find out anything. He was immobile in the center of a time warp. He could go neither backward nor forward.

The smell of baking bread brought him out of his reverie. Mildred was watching him from across the kitchen table. She took his hand. ''It will be fine, really it will.''

''I hope you're right, Mildred. There's something important I need to remember, I just get another headache trying. But I can't, I can't! Dear God, what am I to do?''

''Give it time, Lucas, give it time—and pray,'' she added.

It would all come back to Lucas. He knew that, it had to. He wanted to return to the world, this beautiful, vivid world that for now was closed to him by a heavy gray curtain.

Someday that curtain would rise and give him back his life.

The Virginia & Truckee train ride from Carson City was making Jonathan Woodrow nauseous. Soot from the engine filtered in through the windows as it made the twisting journey up the mountain. The heat was unbearable and the smell of sweating bodies in the

packed train did not make the trip any more pleasant.
Two towheaded boys were running up and down the
aisle, their mother ignoring their antics. A vendor came
through just as Jonathan was about to reprimand the
boys himself. Instead he purchased an apple and a
sandwich. He was famished. The children sat down
and started coaxing their mother to buy them each a
sweet. They were quiet, at least for a while, as they
sat chewing their taffy.

"I hope this darned trip is worth the trouble!" Jonathan thought out loud.

Ahead was Virginia City, and the engineer started
blasting the whistle to announce the train's arrival.
Jonathan was only too glad to stand and stretch his
legs. He lifted his valise down from the rack over his
head and headed for the steps. Standing on the platform, he got his first impression of Virginia City. The
dirt streets, dusty cowboys on horseback, and a Chinese
man pushing a two-wheeled cart down the middle of
the road and trying to dodge horses were the first things
he noticed. The sun beamed down mercilessly. It was
dry and hot. Taking out a soiled handkerchief, he
mopped at his sweaty face.

The conductor was helping two women off the train
as Jonathan approached him.

"Sir, is there transportation into town, and if you
would be so kind, would you recommend a hotel or a
reputable boardinghouse. It would be most appreci-
ated." His voice was like thick syrup.

The conductor took out his pocket watch and
checked the time before he spoke. "Well, there's the

Grand Hotel, but it is expensive and the food, frankly, isn't all that grand! I'd recommend Mrs. Hoffman's boardinghouse. There's a surrey over there. See it, the one with the skinny fella standing beside it smoking a pipe? That's Moses. He can take you there. Mrs. Hoffman keeps a nice place. Tell her Matthew sent you, that's me. She'll treat you right good.''

The engineer signaled that it was time to leave the station, and Jonathan thanked the conductor as he headed for the surrey, Moses, and Mrs. Hoffman's boardinghouse.

Most of all he looked forward to a nice hot bath, and then to business. He would see just what this Hiram Brunswick looked like and what he had to hide, if anything, that might be incriminating. Since he had heard the news that Lucas Forester had gone to San Francisco and never returned, Jonathan would have less to do than originally planned, unless, of course, he ended up going to California too. He doubted that.

He was thinking of this as he left the station and hoped he would find something good to report to Conrad, something that would make this miserable trip from Kansas City worthwhile.

''You're too thin! You have got to eat! How many times have I gotta tell you?'' Clarisa spoke sharply. She knew that somebody had to do something about Agatha, who sat at the kitchen table, head down, just staring at her food.

''It happens! Men are like that, in love with you one

day and off with some other woman the next. Can't trust a dang, blamed one of them!''

Clarisa kept chopping at a large head of cabbage. She was doing it with a vengeance.

''I know it hurts.'' She spoke with sympathy now as she walked over and put a hand on Agatha's shoulder.

''You've just got to eat! Your father and me and Nate, we're all crazy with worry. You gonna put us through this much longer? We'll all die with the worry!''

It was quiet for a few moments and then Agatha spoke.

''I know. I'm sorry. I've put you through so much. Forgive me. I'll try to go on, but Clarisa, it is so hard to forget everything.''

Picking up her fork, she pushed the food around her plate and tried to eat some of it. It all tasted the same— Clarisa's good cooking, but it all tasted the same.

Much later she walked outside, probably for the hundredth time since Lucas had gone. The sun was high in a brilliant blue sky and the air was warm. Agatha found she was standing in the very spot she had been the night that Lucas had declared his love. Tears came again. They washed down her cheeks silently. There were no hysterics, just quiet tears and pain, and a churning in the pit of her stomach so strong that it left a bitter taste in her mouth.

''What can I do, Lucas? I love you. Where are you? Why have you disappeared? Please, please come riding up through the front gate as you did that night. Please, please come back to me!''

But only silence and emptiness filled the front yard. No one was coming up the road.

She turned and walked back into the house.

''Darned heat, darned hard ground, darned barbed wire! Darn everything!''

Nate was in a black mood. The men helping him all looked the other way and kept on working. This wasn't like Nate at all, but it had been this way for weeks on end. Nobody knew the reason and nobody dared to ask.

As the ranch hands rode back at dinnertime, Nate's right-hand man, Jim, held back and rode beside him.

''Boss, I gotta talk to you. I know somethin' is bothering you and if it's none of my business, just say so. But the men are getting a mite testy at the way you're actin'. If any of us can help, well, we would be only too glad to oblige.''

They rode in silence for a while. The wind off the mountains was becoming cooler. Nate took off his hat and shook away the accumulated dust of the hot summer day.

''I guess I have been a mite testy. Sorry.'' He did not smile.

''You got a right to know, but you better keep this to yourself. Just tell the others I ain't been feelin' well.''

They rode again for a while in silence. Off toward

Dayton a huge dust devil was growing as the cooler air hit the baked earth. It loomed large across the sky.

"Well, go on." Jim finally broke the silence.

"It's Miss Agatha. This here fella, named Lucas Forester, he was here awhile back. Seems they fell in love. He left for San Francisco, was supposed to come back here months ago. She got one card from him and not a danged word since! The poor thing is nearly crazy.

"I don't understand it! I really don't! I liked the man. He wasn't the kind to do somethin' like this! There has to be a reason. I know it! I feel it in my gut! But what the blue blazes can I do about it?"

The dust devil came closer, bringing with it a cloud of swirling debris, then it veered away and dissipated in the hills farther on.

"Go find out!" Jim spoke.

"What!"

"Go after that fella and find out! Heck, it's better than sitting here fiddlin' with nothing and driving the ranch hands crazy. You never been a man to sit and do nothing! Go find out!"

Nate rode back with Jim without speaking. He was tired and hungry, and he was miserable about what had been going on at the ranch. He loved Agatha as they all did, and he hated to see her hurting. Jim was right— he had to go.

"You're right, by Jesus! I'm goin'!"

Ike Masterly had written to Hiram asking if he had accepted any offers from the others in reference to the sale of the ranch. Hiram replied that since he had a tentative understanding with Conrad Fillmore, any other bids would have to wait. He had given Conrad a lot of time, but his latest letter said that he was still interested and would Hiram please wait another month for a positive answer. That had been two weeks ago, and although Hiram was anxious, they were very busy both at the ranch and at the bank. The mines were all in full production, the town was crowded with new people, and new buildings were going up faster than anyone would have believed possible. Virginia City was growing.

Hiram had noticed that Agatha was quiet and seemed out of sorts lately but did not know the reason and had been too busy with all the problems pertaining to the sale of the ranch and business at the bank to ask questions.

Nate finally approached his boss about time off. They had been too busy for weeks for him to even think about it before.

''Mr. Brunswick.'' Nate stood, twisting his hat round and round in his hands. ''I need some time off. I know it ain't a good time to ask, but it is important.''

Hiram looked at Nate. He knew this man, knew he would never ask for time off if it wasn't indeed very important.

''It isn't anything that can wait.'' It was not a question.

''No,'' Nate replied reluctantly.

''Well, if you think Jim can take care of things. How much time will you need?''

"A coupla weeks, could be a little more. I'll get back as soon as I can, sooner than two weeks, maybe. Anyway, I'll try."

Much later, Clarisa, who knew exactly where Nate was going—and why—saw a light go on in the barn. Nate was finishing his chores, she could see him moving around, his shadow loomed large by the hay loft door. He would be going to bed soon, then be up before dawn to head for San Francisco. But for Clarisa there would be little sleep, not tonight. Instead she sat for hours in the old rocking chair by her bedroom window, hands clenched tightly together in her lap.

"God help my man, help him find out what happened to Mr. Lucas."

Only then did she realize she had called Nate "my man." She flushed at the thought.

"God bless them all, watch over them too, Lord! They're good people, my Nate, Agatha, Mr. Brunswick, and Mr. Lucas. I love all of them."

Only after her prayer did she finally go to bed and to sleep.

The stars were brilliant tonight, the sky as black as velvet and the moon so bright Agatha could see every bush and flower in the yard etched in shadow. The far-off noise of a herd of wild horses could be heard as they moved through one of the canyons above. Nate was busy in the barn and down the hall she could hear Clarisa settling in for the night. After a while Nate left the barn and Agatha watched his lantern glowing in the dark as he headed for the bunkhouse. Finally all movement and sound stopped. It seemed to Agatha that the whole world had gone to sleep. Except her. Sometime before dawn sleep finally came.

Clarisa woke early. It wasn't five o'clock yet, and the moon was now low in the sky, lighting her room brightly. She got out of bed and dressed by its glow, trying not to make any noise lest she wake Agatha, who she knew would be sleeping lightly, if at all. As she went down the stairs the smell of cooking drifted toward her. There was Nate already in the kitchen making a pot of coffee and frying eggs. The room was chilly and the warmth from the wood stove felt good. She walked up beside him and rubbed her hands together over the fire, trying to warm them. Nate gently put his arm around her shoulders, turned her to face him, and held her in his arms for a moment, then let her go. These two friends needed few words.

"You've got to find him."

"I will, Clarisa. Even if it turns out wrong, she has to know just what's going on."

They sat quietly eating breakfast, each with their own thoughts, as a silken dawn crept slowly into the room.

Nate got up and took his dishes to the sink. He stood for a few moments looking out across the corral.

"I have to go. Clarisa, when I get back, will you marry me? Please," he added finally when she had not answered.

"Yes, you old buzzard. You know danged right well I will!" She was crying.

The morning sky had blushed a brilliant pink. Clarisa watched Nate as he rode away with Jim across the front pasture and out through the gate. After a few moments dust from the wagon was all that could be seen, and then it too disappeared. She turned from where she stood at the front door, went back into the kitchen, and started washing up. Another day had begun.

As Nate was boarding the train, Mrs. Hoffman was busy feeding her tenants at the boardinghouse.

"Would you pass the potatoes, please, Miss Gibson?"

The young woman looked up, frowned, and pushed the plate toward Jonathan.

"Mrs. Hoffman, when breakfast is finished, would you please direct me to the bank, and also I need to go to the courthouse, the Hall of Records, to be exact."

"Which bank, Mr. Woodrow—the Comstock, the Virginia, or the new bank, forgot its name?"

"I do believe my friend told me to go to the Virginia bank."

"Well, the courthouse is up on B Street, and the bank is just behind it. You can't miss it. If you have any questions there, see Victor. Mr. Brunswick is the president, but Victor is the head teller. A very efficient man."

Breakfast was over by eight and Jonathan left the boardinghouse and walked around the town. Most of the saloons were quiet, a few men were gambling, fewer yet drinking this early in the day. At the Silver Queen a piano player was already banging away at an old upright, its tinny sound vibrating all the way out into the street. Jonathan enjoyed the sound of it and the unusual feeling of the wooden sidewalk that moved a little as he walked along, looking over the town. Miniature Victorian cottages lined the outskirts of town, an attempt at making this look a little more Eastern, a little less like a mining town. It gave the area a unique look of its own. The whole atmosphere was pleasant and different.

By eight o'clock the courthouse was open and he spent the morning going through the tax records, assessments, and deeds. It was a tedious job, this hunting up the property values and recorded wealth of one Hiram Brunswick. By one o'clock he was finished and had a quick lunch at a little restaurant on a side street. A short walk toward the center of town brought him to the Virginia Bank, where he entered, asked for Victor, and was escorted to a small room toward the back of the building. On the way they passed the vault. It was the latest and best on the market—absolutely soundproof. A bank robber would have a rough time getting into that vault.

Victor was very solicitous. "Sir, how may I assist you?"

"I'm new in town. I've been thinking of transferring my money from my bank in the East to an establishment in Virginia City. There seems to be a lot going on here and I am thinking about starting a business, that is, if all goes according to plan."

"That's wonderful, Mr., uh, what was your name again? Forgive me, sir, I have been so busy all day. Names keep slipping away."

"Jonathan Woodrow. And I understand perfectly. No insult taken."

Victor gave him the figures he had requested, talked to him a few moments, and found it reasonably easy to discharge Mr. Woodrow from his company. He didn't like the man, and he didn't know why. It was probably the grating voice, his oily manner, or the way his eyes shifted around as he talked and never settled on any one thing. Not once had he looked Victor directly in the eye.

"Thank you, Mr. Beecham—Victor, is it? Do you mind if I call you that?" His words were accompanied by a fine spray of saliva.

"Not at all, Mr. Woodrow, not at all," Victor replied, all the while cringing at the thought of even a remote familiarity with this man.

Jonathan started out of the bank. Just as he got to the door he noticed a gentleman coming out of the door marked PRESIDENT. He had a quiet air and was rather handsome with brown hair, a full beard and mustache, and deep-set eyes. It was the eyes that he noticed most. They seemed to stare through Jonathan all the way to the back of his head. He didn't know why, but it was unsettling. *Odd,* he thought. *I swear, no that's not possible, I've never been here before. But I could swear that I've seen that man before.*

And Hiram, who had seen Jonathan all too clearly, was absolutely certain he had seen him before. Moving back into his office, he sat heavily in his chair behind his huge desk. He had just seen the one man in this entire world he had never, ever wanted to set eyes on again.

Hiram put his head down heavily on the desk. He reached inside the top drawer, fumbled in the back for his pillbox and finally managed to extract one to put under his tongue.

The pain in his chest diminished and he spoke aloud.

"God help me, dear God, help me!"

Chapter Eight

Nate looked with wonder out of the window at the California scenery. He had never traveled outside of Nevada, and while anxious about finding Lucas Forester, he was still enjoying the trip.

"Sacramento, we're coming into Sacramento!" the conductor announced loudly. The clicking of the rails was even louder as he opened each of the doors to pass from one car to the other.

Nate got out of the train, excusing himself as he pushed pass people who were boarding. There were a lot of them—children, old folks, men in fancy suits, all sorts of people. Valises were being hauled into the mail car along with boxes and sacks of mail.

Nate was in awe of all the activity going on everywhere at the station. All he had time to do was get a cup of coffee and return to his seat before the train started again. A newly arrived passenger sitting directly behind Nate began to settle himself and, as the train lurched forward, accidentally pushed Nate's seat forward. The unexpected movement caused some of his coffee to spill down into his lap.

"Darn!" Nate exclaimed, standing.

"Oh, sir, I am so sorry. Here, take this." He handed Nate a huge, white scarf.

"It's OK, I wouldn't want to dirty that fine scarf."

"Sir, I insist!" And with this the man came forward and sat beside Nate.

"This traveling is an abomination! Especially in the summer. I am from Maine, clear up near the border of Canada and close to the ocean. The sea breezes keep us reasonably cool, which is, perhaps, why I find this heat so difficult to handle. But then people say we New Englanders are an odd lot anyway." He laughed.

"I never heard tell any such thing. But then I ain't ever been out of Nevada before. You talk kinda nice-soundin' to me." Nate was busy wiping off the coffee with his own checkered handkerchief.

"What a nice thing to say. Sir, I am Jeremy Wilcox, of the Wilcox Lumber Company, Bangor, Maine. And you, sir, may I inquire as to your name?"

"Me! I'm Nathan P. Culpepper, people call me Nate. I work for Hiram Brunswick, he's a banker in town. I'm the foreman at his ranch."

"And where would you be heading, if I may ask?"

"Goin' to San Francisco. Have to look for a friend of the family. It's a long story. It is gonna be somethin', lookin' for a needle in a haystack. But I gotta try."

"Well, Nate, I too am going to the city. I shall be glad to assist you in any way that I can. Do you have a place to stay?"

"Hadn't thought much about it. Imagine I'll look for a hotel somewhere."

"Well then, I can take care of that. My sister married a seaman from San Francisco. She runs a small, not fancy, but very clean boardinghouse. That's where I am going. I'm certain we can find a nice room for you at a reasonable rate. You will really enjoy it, it's right by the water. That's if you wish. Sally will be only too glad to show you a room. If it isn't to your liking there will be no hard feelings."

"Well, now," Nate replied, "that sure is kindly of you, Mr. Wilcox."

The two new friends spent the rest of the trip talking. Mr. Wilcox enjoyed this rugged Westerner. It had been an arduous trip until now, but Nate brought to life tales of the West. Time flew by, and before too long the train was coming into San Francisco. Nate sat looking out the window, entranced. For hours he had all but forgotten just why he was making this journey, but at the sight of the city it all returned. He remembered Lucas Forester and just exactly why he was here.

Clarisa was trying to keep the household together. First there was the problem with Agatha not eating, not visiting her friends, not doing anything but staring into space. The girl was almost ill. Now it was Mr. Brunswick. He had become short tempered and just pushed his food around his plate too. And then, after

getting up from the dinner table with the food untouched, he would go into the parlor and walk up and
down like a caged animal, or stand by the fireplace
smoking a cigar, rubbing his chest and staring at nothing. What was happening? She sat down at the kitchen
table, put her head in her hands, and cried. She hadn't
done that in twenty years.

"God help me, please Lord! I don't know where to
turn! Help Nate find out somethin' and get home before
I go crazy. Tell me what to do, please tell me what to
do!"

The empty kitchen windows only stared back at her.
The air was as still as death and outside the tumbleweed
and sage had dried to a crisp in hot desert air.

Standing, she tried to get back to preparing dinner.
It seemed of little use, nobody would eat anything. But
she had to try.

Everyone was quiet at the bank. A tension had de-
veloped, with Victor wringing his hands at Hiram's
behavior. It filtered down to the tellers. There was
something wrong, it was in the air.

Hiram had just sent his head teller back to his office.
There was a problem that he should have handled;
instead he told Victor to do what he thought best. He
couldn't think, couldn't do anything until he knew for
certain that Jonathan Woodrow had left town.

Standing up, he moved to a large armchair usually
kept for customers. He sat down, his body bent over,
his head lowered, his hands clasped tightly together.
The chair felt so deep it almost seemed to swallow

him. For days he had been having headaches, his eyes seemed not to focus, and his stomach churned. A new headache was coming on and with it a terrible stabbing pain in his chest that began to move down his arm. The pain became worse and he rose and moved brokenly toward his desk. At that moment, returning to Hiram's office, Victor walked into the room and watched horrified as Hiram, eyes unseeing, face ashen, hands clutching his chest, fell to the floor.

A sudden summer storm was boiling its way across the Sierra Nevada. The wind was whistling through the desert sage and rattling every window in Virginia City. Jonathan had trouble seeing with all the sand blowing through the air. He was trying to find his way to the office of the Comstock Saloon. His investigation of Hiram was almost complete. There wasn't anything to be found in the least incriminating. Hiram's personal life seemed void of the usual associations. Outside of being friends with some of Virginia City's civic leaders, he seemed to just stay at home on his ranch. Jonathan knew of no women in Hiram's life and found that most peculiar. All that he did discover was that he was a widower, but no one, anywhere, seemed to know where or when his wife had died. But the one point that was so exasperating to Jonathan was that he could find nothing about the man's life before he had come to Virginia City. That part of the man's life was a blank page! Before arriving in this desert town, Hiram Brunswick seemed not to have existed! Jonathan found this exciting. When anyone had a blank space in his history it could mean only one thing—he had something to hide.

"Sir, may I assist you?" The question came from a young man at the bar, which at this early hour was empty of customers.

"I'm looking for a Mr. Conway, the owner, I believe."

"He won't be in for a couple of hours. Can I help?"

"No, but if you have any coffee, I would like a cup."

The bartender obliged, and Jonathan sat looking at all of the usual paraphernalia that always seems to be present in every saloon in the world—bottles of every description, glasses, pictures, posters. Jonathan wasn't anxious to return to the street while the wind was blowing so fiercely. Instead he drank his coffee while moving around the room looking at the many pictures that covered the walls. In one section he found a board covered with items of local information, want ads, things for sale, and several pictures. On one picture someone had added a mustache and beard to the face of an otherwise beautiful young woman. He stood staring at it for a long time, wondering just what it was about the picture that piqued his interest. He could not shake the feeling there was something he should remember that would not surface. There was something there—a thought, a remembrance, a clue to something! What was it?

Finishing his coffee, he left the saloon and wandered down the street toward the cemetery. He thought perhaps he would find a tombstone that said "Brunswick.'' Certainly a man could not live in a community this long and not have something to hide. Even if people had assured him that Hiram's wife had not died in Virginia City, perhaps they were wrong. The wind had risen in intensity. Leaves and dead flowers left on graves were blowing everywhere. It started to rain. Jonathan stood, unseeing, before a tombstone with a huge carved angel at its base. He pulled the collar of his coat tightly up around his neck and let the rain run down his face. There was something he should remember, something he had seen in the saloon. Why wouldn't it come to him? He felt like a man trying to put his arms around a shadow. There was substance there, but it was just outside of his reach. In desperation at his inability to find the answer, he started walking back toward town, his head down against the wind, his shoulders wet with the rain, and then suddenly he knew what it was about the picture on the wall at the Comstock Saloon that had drawn his interest. Don't add a mustache and beard to a picture, take them away! What did that leave?

Jonathan walked the rest of the way back to Mrs. Hoffman's boardinghouse and never noticed that the rain was coming down harder than ever and that he was now soaking wet.

He had his answer. It wasn't what you have when you added a mustache and beard to a face, it was what you have when you take away a mustache and beard. . . .

You have Hiram Brunswick's past!

* * *

The usual smell of ether and medicine hung heavily in the hospital corridor air. Agatha did not notice. She had been helping Lizbeth can fruit when Victor found her. She had not understood what Victor had said over the noise of the chattering children. She was trying to keep busy and not think about Lucas. Going to help her friend had seemed a good idea. It had taken several attempts for Victor to finally get her attention and only when he had grabbed her bodily and pulled her out of the steamy room and into the pouring rain did she understand that something was wrong.

"It's your father, Agatha! It looks like a heart attack. Hurry, please hurry, it doesn't look good."

Agatha could scarcely believe her ears or her eyes. Victor was crying. He was actually crying and for a single moment she found this astonishing. It was only then that what he had come to say had finally penetrated her thoughts and washed away Lucas and Lizbeth and everything else. Her father could be dying.

When she finally found his room Agatha could not believe the man lying on those white sheets could be her father. This man looked twenty years older than Hiram Brunswick. It was hours later that he finally opened his eyes and looked up at his daughter.

"Bridie!" he said.

"Father," she said gently, "it's me, Agatha."

"No," he answered and, struggling for breath, he continued.

"Your name is Bridie."

*　　*　　*

Doctor Miles Jacobson had been a friend of the family since their arrival in Nevada. It was Jake, as everyone called him, who sewed up gunshot wounds, delivered babies, and gave advice. At this moment, he was wondering at the fortitude of Hiram Brunswick. The man should be dead.

Leaving the emergency room of the hospital, he took a deep breath, picked up his morning coat from a chair in the hallway, put it on, grabbed again his ever-present black bag, and moved slowly toward the waiting room where Agatha had been waiting for hours. His face was haggard from lack of sleep. He was surprised to see the light of dawn coming through the windows. He had been at Hiram's bedside all night long.

"Jake!" It was all that Agatha could say.

"Well, it isn't good; but it isn't all bad. He's had a heart attack. A bad one. But your father has an amazing constitution. However, from now on he absolutely must take it easy, very easy. And watch his diet. No more cigars, not too much drinking, just an occasional glass of sherry. If he does what he's told—and you must see to it that he does—he should live a normal life."

He smiled and sat down heavily on a worn divan.

"I gave him a sedative. He should sleep a good eight hours. I'll be back late this afternoon. In the meantime I've ordered nurses around the clock.

"It's time you were told." Jake stopped for a moment and looked away from Agatha. He folded his hands together in a tight grip and rubbed the palms together. He leaned forward and spoke again.

"Hiram didn't want you to know. He's had a heart problem for some time now and has medication. Make sure that he carries it with him at all times or has it close by. If he feels an attack coming on he is to place a pill under his tongue immediately! He's had several bad times recently and for the life of me I don't know why, but he seems to be upset about something. Something he isn't telling me, anyway. Do you have any idea what it could be?"

"No. Not unless it is trying to sell the ranch. It isn't money, Jake, nothing like that, but one thing does bother me, something that happened just after he regained consciousness for that short time last night."

"What?"

"He called me Bridie! When I said no, it's Agatha, he answered, 'No, you're Bridie'!"

Jake started to say something but stopped. Several moments passed before he answered and Agatha had the feeling that Jake was holding something back.

"Just hallucinations, that's all. I wouldn't worry about it too much. When I finally release him see if, for once in his life, he can learn to take it easy! If he doesn't, well, I cannot be responsible. It's up to him and you to see that he lives as long as he should. Who else will I have to beat at chess?" He smiled.

"Jake, how can I thank you?"

Clarisa had been sitting quietly, waiting—and praying. Finally she spoke. "He'll do as he's told! I'll see to that. Now if you can get Miss Agatha to eat and behave herself, maybe we can get them both better at the same time."

"And you, young lady, you do as Clarisa says! You go home and get some sleep. And eat something! You look terrible! Now that's an order. There's nothing else you can do here."

"I just want to stay a little longer. Clarisa, you can go, but send Jim back for me in an hour or so."

"Done!" Clarisa said, relief showing on her tired face.

Jake ran a hand over his tired face. "Just remember, Agatha, your father has been the best friend I have ever had. What am I saying! You know that. Things are never easy for a country doctor, at least they weren't for me. If it hadn't been for Hiram, Marie and I wouldn't have that nice house on the hill. Miners and drunkards don't always pay their bills. I haven't forgotten, I never will.

"Well, I have to head back downtown again. There's a little lady friend of yours about to have another baby."

"Lizbeth? I was just with her yesterday! I was there when Victor found me. It's a little early, isn't it?"

"Yes," Jake said. "But don't worry, that's to be expected with this one, she'll be fine."

"Oh, I'm so glad. I'll be in with my father until Jim comes back for me, Jake, so please let me know when it's all over. I've been neglecting her. See if there is anything Clarisa can do. Is that all right, Clarisa?"

"You got it. Maybe I should have Jim take me down to Lizbeth's first before I go home. I'll watch those little ones. Jim can keep us all in touch."

Agatha watched as Clarisa rushed out to Jim, who

was sleeping in the back of the buckboard. All she saw of Jake was his back as he moved hurriedly toward the door to Lizbeth's, where a new life was about to make its way into the world.

And then she remembered Lucas, and the agony of wondering what had happened to him began again.

Chapter Nine

Conrad Fillmore arrived unannounced at Mrs. Hoffman's boardinghouse. He was looking for Jonathan Woodrow. Pearl didn't know where he was, but invited Conrad for dinner. It had been much too long since his last inquiry had gone unanswered. He was paying this man for results, not silence. Excusing himself, he began a search of all the saloons—and everywhere else in town that Jonathan could be visiting. The rain from yesterday's downpour had left huge puddles in the street that wagons and horses had churned into seas of mud. A mining wagon went past Conrad. One of its wheels went down into a huge chuckhole, splattering his new boots and soiling his suit. He was furious. Scraping at his filthy clothes, he headed into the nearest barbershop to try and clean up. There sat the elusive Jonathan getting a shave.

"Well, look who's here," Jonathan said, obviously surprised and not too pleased. He wasn't ready yet for Conrad. There were two ways to look at what he knew. He could tell his employer and get paid for his time spent in his investigation, or he could try and use the information to his own advantage. The latter seemed the right thing to do. It was simply a matter of figuring out how. In that quick moment, as he looked up and saw Conrad, his decision was made. He would wait and figure an angle. If nothing surfaced there was still time to profit from his information. After all, what was the rush? Maybe Conrad figured he didn't have much time, but Jonathan had the upper hand. He was the person who knew who Hiram Brunswick was, and why his past had been hidden, Conrad didn't! The man could darned well wait.

"When you are finished, and I've cleaned up my clothes, we need to talk. Meet me at the Bucket of Blood, out on the balcony in back. And don't keep me waiting!"

With those words spoken, Conrad moved to the back of the shop where a sign said BATHS. He didn't need a bath, just a chance to clean off his clothes. When he had finished he found Jonathan had already left for their meeting. He wasn't about to take any guff from this man, he was sick and tired of waiting for some communication. There had to be something he had found. Nobody in the world was perfect. Of that, Conrad was certain. He squared his shoulders and in long, deliberate strides walked down the street and entered the Bucket of Blood Saloon.

* * *

Nate and Jeremy Wilcox had become friends quickly. While Jeremy was a rather pompous fellow, he had a heart of gold and really enjoyed his new "partner in crime," as he set out with Nate to find Lucas Forester. At the moment they were enjoying the evening air and watching the boats and ships in the harbor. Jeremy had tilted his chair back and had his feet up on the wooden banister that surrounded his sister's back porch. He was twirling a cigar between his lips. The cigar's light had gone out an hour before. It had been a long day.

"You two want coffee?" Sally had come through the screen door, wiping her hands on a towel.

"That would be nice," Nate replied. "I really would enjoy a cup of coffee. Can I help?"

"Just set yourself right where you are, no guest of mine works in this house, just freeloaders like my brother!"

Jeremy turned and frowned. "Well!"

They all had to laugh. Sally was thrilled that her brother had finally come to visit. They hadn't seen each other for a long, long time.

Sally brought out their coffee and sat with Nate and her brother while they enjoyed the cool evening air.

"We will need to go in soon, it does get cold some nights. I've seen it blow here so hard and the air turn so cold that your ears feel like tin!"

They were quiet for a while, and then Jeremy spoke.

"Tomorrow we have to go into town and check the city directory. They aren't updated, but they did a census a few years back, there might be something. We've tried everything else I can think of, outside of up on the roof and screaming Lucas Forester's name. But anything else you can think of, Nate, I'll be only too pleased to assist. I know how difficult this has been for you. Our choice of places to inquire are dwindling, I'm afraid.''

''Jeremy, I don't know what I would have done without you. Here I was a person you hardly knew, and you took me in and helped so much. Tell you what, when Clarisa and I get married, I want you to come and be my best man.''

''Sir, I would be most honored. What a nice thing for you to say. I am so anxious to meet your fiancée. She sounds lovely, just lovely.''

''Well, that's not exactly the word I would use for Clarisa! A little too feisty for that. But under that shell there hides a heart of pure gold.'' Nate laughed. ''But I love her, temper and all!''

Night had finally come to San Francisco, and with it a dense fog that stifled all sound except that of a foghorn bleating its mournful message out across the water. It fitted Luke's mood. The doctors had told him his limp would probably be permanent. The scars on his head were now covered with newly grown hair. Occasionally he would have a headache, but they were decreasing in intensity and coming with less frequency. It would soon be time for him to get out and search for his identity. But approval had not yet been given and, while he was anxious to begin, he knew his limitations. Even a short walk left him exhausted. His patience was all but gone and yet he was helpless.

"Here, dear, let me fix your feet. That stool is off too far to one side." Mildred was trying as hard as she could to make him comfortable, trying to understand exactly what Lucas was going through.

"I brought home three new books for you to read; patients keep leaving them at the hospital. They've all been read by the nurses and they wanted you to have them. They should keep you busy for a while."

"Thanks, I feel like this is such an imposition on you. I just don't think I will ever be able to thank you enough, Mildred. I didn't know there were people like you left in the world." And then Lucas laughed. "How would I know what people are like in the world, I haven't any world!"

"Well, you will, Lucas, and when you find it you will be filthy rich and buy me all kinds of baubles and bangles! How does that sound?"

"It sounds great," he answered, but in his heart he wondered. And kept on wondering, day, after day, after day. If he didn't remember something tangible soon, he would go crazy!

Three days later, as Lucas was headed to the hospital for yet another doctor's examination, Nate, accompanied by Jeremy, was moving toward San Francisco's railroad station to return to Virginia City. Going down a crowded city street two hansom cabs passed each other traveling in different directions.

Nate and Lucas had been only a few feet apart.

*   *   *

Nate dreaded being back in Virginia City. He knew how terrible Clarisa was going to feel that he had failed to find Lucas or, for that matter, any trace of him. Neither of them had told Agatha what they were doing. It would be difficult for him to lie; it just wasn't in him, but he would have to try. She had to think he had been away on his own personal business, and he hadn't yet even tried to make up a story.

The train pulled to a stop, its smokestack puffing in long, slow, noisy sighs, and black soot billowed out, drifting skyward into the bright Nevada sky.

Nate looked out at the familiar sights that had been a big part of his adult life. Horses were moving slowly down the street ridden by the same dusty cowboys that always seemed to be coming into or leaving town. The sound of people walking on the wooden sidewalk was as familiar as the sound of Clarisa's voice. He wanted so much to be happy about coming home, but he was unhappy at his failure.

He stood for a moment still watching everything, then shifted his valise from one hand to the other, pulled his hat forward to shade his eyes from the late afternoon sun, and moved ahead. What was awaiting him at Brunswick Manor had to be faced. It was as simple as that, and Nate Culpepper was a man who always faced his responsibilities, good or bad.

The buckboard was stopped by the side of the station filled with supplies and a tired-looking Jim sitting up on the seat watching Nate come down from the platform. Maybe it wouldn't be as bad as he thought. The air was so clear and clean and the warm sun welcome after the cool, damp weather that had chilled his bones in San Francisco. At least he would be seeing Clarisa again and maybe they could make plans to get married soon. It might even help Agatha to have something to think about other than Lucas.

"Hi!" Jim greeted him.

"Hi! Wish I had something good to report. I don't, so don't ask!"

"I wasn't gonna!" was the reply.

The two friends rode back toward the ranch as twilight settled on the horizon and a huge orange sun slowly dipped behind the mountains.

"Made a couple of new friends. I'll tell you all about it when we get out doin' the fencin', but right now I'm just tired. How's Clarisa and Agatha?"

"Well, I wasn't gonna worry you yet. They're fine, so relax, but the boss had a heart attack."

"He had what?"

"Well, he's home now, but he has to take it easy. Looks like he'll have to sell the ranch for sure. He won't be allowed back to work for a week or more yet, and even then he will have to take it easy. Victor is holdin' down the fort. For the present, anyway, that's what I hear tell."

"Good God, it ain't enough on Agatha and Clarisa, this too!"

"Tell the truth, it has given Miss Agatha something else to think about besides Lucas. She's been too busy taking care of her father to think much about her other problems. At least it seems like she is."

"Well, that's something good, leastways!"

The two men were quiet as Jim drove the team up from town over the familiar road with the same familiar and anticipated ruts. Nate looked toward the last hill that shielded Brunswick Manor from town. Clarisa would be waiting for him, and the trouble that had haunted them would still be there, now made even worse by Mr. Brunswick's illness. All he wanted at this moment was to hold Clarisa tightly in his arms and shut out everything sad that was hurting them and those they loved. For now that would have to be enough.

The ranch was just ahead and Nate could see Clarisa sitting on the veranda looking their way as they rode up to the corral. She watched as Nate got down and headed toward her. She looked tired.

"Don't say a thing," she whispered in his ear as he hugged her to his bony frame.

"She's just inside the door. Thinks you been visiting a sister. I sure do hope you can lie. Jim, tell you about Mr. Brunswick?" She added the last as they headed arm in arm toward the kitchen door.

"Yep, darn shame. On top of everything else. God, I am ever glad to see you!"

He turned toward Clarisa and smiled. A wan and tired smile, for that was all that he could muster.

"Whatever has happened to the good life we used to have here?" he asked.

"It will come again. It will, I promise. You didn't find out anything, did you?"

"No." It was all that he could say.

"No need to be ashamed. You did what you could. Nobody could ask for more. I love you for that."

The meeting between Jonathan Woodrow and Conrad Fillmore the week before had not gone well. In his usual brusque way, Conrad had torn into Jonathan with questions. His nostrils flared and his eyes squinted when he lost control of his temper. Both movements were evident in his conversation at the Bucket of Blood Saloon. Jonathan's reaction was to dig in his heels and become even more determined to wait out any decision about his astonishing discovery. It really didn't matter to him now if Conrad ever paid him for his investigation, the realization of Hiram Brunswick's true worth, and the possibilities it presented, were far more valuable than any pittance from Conrad. He could wait. It had all become very academic when the news had spread through town that the president of the Virginia Bank had had a heart attack. Nothing could be done for a while. He would have to wait. At least, Jonathan reasoned, until the man was at home for a time and recovered to some extent.

Looking back at his discovery, it was easy to see why no one in Virginia City knew anything about Hiram prior to his arrival in town with his tiny daughter in tow. It was also understandable since so many people of unknown origin had come here to start a new life. No one pried. It was an unspoken code around the mines and in the towns that were supported by the gold and silver that had changed the face of the West.

Jonathan thought about this while waiting to hear

that Hiram had recovered sufficiently to return to the bank. Only then would he make his move. In the meantime he had to get Conrad Fillmore out of town; he knew the man well enough to realize that Conrad would certainly know something was not exactly right, or at the very least, that Jonathan was indeed lying. He was taking a risk, he knew that, for Hiram could take a turn for the worse, have another attack, and die. That would leave Jonathan with nothing. He would have to take that risk. The stakes were high and he knew it.

A week later the two men met just outside of town, on a hill looking down toward Gold City. Jonathan had walked and was winded, Conrad sat astride a beautiful mare and was looking down at the man he had employed.

That man always seems to get the best out of every situation, Jonathan thought as he approached the big man with that head of pure white hair. *Has the world by the tail, the pompous son of a gun!* The wide smile on his face was in complete contrast to his thoughts.

Conrad slipped off the saddle with the grace of a true horseman, the leather making a soft, squeaking sound as he slid to the ground.

"Well," he asked, "do you have any news, or don't you?"

Conrad was going to be very unhappy.

"Really, Mr. Fillmore, I cannot find anything that would be of any value."

"Just what the hell does that mean, anything of value?" He emphasized the word *value*.

"Well, I wonder about his not ever having married

again. There are no women in his life. I find that peculiar. But other than that the man is as pure as my mother's heart.''

Conrad snorted at that last remark.

"Really, Conrad, was that necessary?" He had returned to calling him by his given name.

Ignoring Jonathan's reply, Conrad grabbed at his horse's reins and jerked the animal toward him. The mare shied and moved sideways, shaking her head.

"Hold it, whoa!" He finally settled the horse and moved up into the saddle in one quick movement.

"I'm leaving town on the next available train. Send a bill to my office in Kansas City."

Without another word he turned and put the mare into a full gallop, leaving Jonathan standing alone amid the dry grass and sand, his hat in his hand and a smile that was really a snicker on his face.

"I'll be in touch if I find out anything later."

Jonathan was shouting at the departing figure. If Conrad had heard the words he made no move to show it—he simply rode his horse even harder back toward town.

Lizbeth Roberts was at home with her new baby, a fat little boy named Jacob. It had been a difficult delivery and she was glad to have company, which, she said, gave her an excuse to sit down for a few moments.

"He is absolutely beautiful!" Agatha exclaimed, looking down into the round, pink face.

Jacob was trying to focus his eyes on this new person, and a tiny smiled appeared as he moved his head. Agatha was enchanted.

"It is so good to see you, Agatha. We've all been worried about you, especially with your father so ill. I hear he is doing well. I hope that's true."

Lizbeth kept talking without waiting for any answer. It was her style, and Agatha loved her for all of her chatter and whimsical ways. Right now she needed a friend, someone to talk to, if even for a little while.

"Is Clarisa watching him now? I do hope you didn't leave him alone."

"No, silly, of course Clarisa is watching him. And there is other news. She and Nate are going to be married."

"Well, it's about time! When did they wake up and decide all this? I can hardly wait! Are you going to be the maid of honor? Where will it be, when will it be?"

"Wait a minute, one question at a time. It won't be for a month, it will be a very quiet ceremony at the house with the new Presbyterian minister presiding, and yes, I will be the maid of honor!"

"Darn, I wish it was going to be your wedding!" Lizbeth said and then turned scarlet with embarrassment. "Oh my God, Agatha, I am sorry, really I am! Me and my big mouth." She turned and looked out the window and then back at her friend.

"He'll be back, you wait and see! Nobody could stay away from you this long without there being a good reason. He said he loved you, he proposed, darn it, he will be back!"

Agatha stayed long enough to help Lizbeth with the

children and some canning. The garden had been plentiful with all the hot weather they had been having. Agatha was glad to be busy and away from Brunswick Manor. For the moment she could put everything else aside and simply concentrate on cutting string beans and packing jars. Anything was better than the pain she had been living with for months.

Lizbeth was chattering on about something, Agatha only half listening. She thought again about Lucas, she could not help it, he was always there somewhere in her thoughts.

I wonder just where you are? Those same unspoken words.

At that very moment a train heading for Kansas City was traveling east through Carson City, Nevada. One of its passengers was Lucas Forester.

Chapter Ten

The day had finally arrived for Hiram to return to the bank. He was feeling a good deal better. Jake had given his approval with the promise that he would only stay half days and give as much of his work to Victor as was possible.

"It sure is mighty good to have you up and around!" Nate said as they were riding into town.

"Thank you, Nathan. You have no idea just how great it feels. I have had enough of sitting around and doing nothing for as long as I ever want to! It will be great to be back working at the bank," he replied.

People waved and shouted at Hiram as the surrey moved through town. He hadn't realized just how many friends he had, how many kind and thoughtful people there were in Virginia City. In spite of himself he laughed out loud. It was not his usual demeanor. He wasn't in the habit of waving to people on the street. Somehow it felt good.

One thing he made note of immediately: He had not seen or heard anything about Jonathan Woodrow since just before his heart attack. Without making a fuss about it, he had asked Victor to keep him informed if the man returned to the bank. There had been nothing to report. Hiram hoped his instincts were right and the man had gone. It was, after all, a long time ago and Philadelphia was a good distance away. Maybe it had just been his imagination.

"Good morning, Mr. Brunswick!" The bank employees were all standing at the front door as he entered. A huge banner was draped across the entrance to his office. It said, "Welcome Back!"

Hiram was astonished! He really had no idea that his employees felt anything this friendly toward their employer, and he found his eyes misting. It was embarrassing.

"Thank you, thank you all very much," he said as he headed quickly toward the door to his private office. Victor followed him inside and sat down in front of the desk.

"Well," he said, "you are back. It is really good to see you. You look much better than you did when I was out to see you last week. Marjorie sends her best."

Victor was carrying a huge folder of business papers and for the next few hours the men kept busy with catching up on the problems at the bank. They were interrupted close to lunchtime by a knock on the door. Hiram's secretary spoke.

"There's a gentleman here to see Mr. Brunswick. Says it's important."

"Just a minute," Victor said. "I'll be out." Picking up the last of the folders, he moved toward the door. "I'll see if I can take care of this; if not, do you want to see anyone today?"

"Certainly. I may as well get back into business as usual. You have had your hands full for weeks and I appreciate all that you've done. I do have to get back to work. I can't let you do everything forever."

Victor left the office and returned in a few moments.

"I'm afraid this is something you will need to handle. It's that man you had me keeping an eye open for. A Mr. Woodrow—he insists on talking to no one else but you."

Hiram sat silently in his chair. He looked down at his desk and shuffled a few papers around and said nothing. His heart seemed to jump through his chest.

"Well, what do you want me to do? I can send him away if you like."

"No," Hiram replied. "This I will have to handle myself."

Victor left reluctantly. He knew Hiram, knew him well. Something was wrong, very, very wrong. But there was nothing, at the moment, that he could do about it, not without knowing the reason for Hiram's strange behavior. He moved out of the room. A few moments later he returned and announced Jonathan

Woodrow. Then he turned and left, quietly shutting the door.

"Hello, Hezekiah. It is Hezekiah Bowman, is it not?"

He moved across the room. His eyes never left Hiram's face.

"It's been a long time, almost twenty years, isn't it? What's wrong, Hezekiah, don't remember me? Well, I remember you. Do I ever remember you!"

Finally he sat in the chair beside Hiram's desk. He was looking directly at him, his face only inches away. Jonathan's eyes were cold black shadows that showed nothing. But inside his heart there was only one thing: greed.

The young woman behind the counter was flustered by Lucas Forester. She thought him quite handsome.

"Sir, what can I do for you?"

"I would like to look through a city directory, if you have one available. There's someone I am looking for and would like to check the name, if possible."

"Just who is it you are looking for, sir?"

"Me," Lucas replied, much to her amazement.

"I beg your pardon, sir, did you say you were looking for yourself?" Her eyes opened wide in surprise.

"I'm sorry, I didn't mean to confuse you. Would you please look under the name of Forester, Lucas Forester. I need an address, if that's possible."

"One moment, I'll see what I can find."

After a few moments she returned with a huge book. It seemed all she could do to even carry it.

"Oh, I am sorry, Here, let me help you."

Lucas tried to take the book from her hands, but instead they carried it between them, the young woman never taking her eyes from his face. He tried not to notice.

"I think I can manage to look this up myself, but thank you."

The young woman left, still smiling at this handsome stranger, but Lucas had already started looking through the directory. He found nothing at first, but decided to check under different spellings than what he had assumed was correct. There he found what he had waited months to see, his name in print, and beside it an address. He shouted "At last!" The same young lady looked over at him, astonishment on her face, but Lucas rushed past her without so much as a glance.

The journey had been strenuous. The days on the train had been difficult for him. There was still a great deal of pain, especially in his left leg, and his limp had increased as the trip progressed. However, his headaches were less severe and only seemed to occur when he tried to read for too long a time. Then, at last, what he had hoped for for so long had happened. He could stand any pain and discomfort now, for there was some hope, something to give him a clue as to just who he was and what kind of a life he had lost. He was standing at the door to what may very well be his home. They had found a key in his pocket; that—and some loose change—was all the hospital personnel had found. His billfold had been missing. It was one of the reasons he had so few clues. If not for Mildred

Rainey, he wouldn't even be this far along in his search for his identity.

Lucas walked up the white marble steps and pulled the door chime. Nothing happened. No one came. Taking the key from his pocket, he put it in the lock. It turned in his hand. He walked inside and stood in the foyer. Looking to the right he could see what was obviously a library. By the fireplace was a large, comfortable-looking lounge chair, the kind a man would want to sink into after a long day. Books lined the shelves, and Lucas moved back and forth checking the titles. One whole section was devoted to horsemanship and the raising of cattle. Mildred was right, he was indeed a rancher of some kind.

The house was small but adequate. It was settled in a quiet section of the town, surrounded by trees. Lucas guessed there were two or three acres. All in all, it was a very pleasant surprise. The kitchen had the look of a woman's touch. He wondered just who had taken care of things in his absence. There were a few tins of food, but nothing else to show any recent occupancy.

The parlor had the look of having never been used, or if so, very little, which, all things considered, did not surprise him. He climbed the stairs to the second floor. At the top was a room—obviously his own. It had that look of masculinity everywhere. On a dresser there was a picture of a man and woman with a young boy. The resemblance was undeniable. It was Lucas as a young man. He moved on through the room. A small desk sat directly in front of a window that looked out

into the trees, and as he approached it he saw an en-
velope addressed to him. Opening it, he read

Dear Mr. Forester:

*I thought you were only going to be gone
a couple of weeks. It has been well over a
month since you left. I was worried and sent
a letter to your aunt's house. No answer
came back and I didn't know where else to
write. You were supposed to be there and
somewhere in Nevada, but I didn't know
where. That's a big place to hunt for somebody. Like a needle in a haystack, I'm thinking. Since you haven't returned I have
decided to go home and wait to hear from
you. Get in touch when you return. If I don't
hear from you soon I will need to seek other
employment.*

Sincerely yours, Katie.

It was dated months before.

Lucas spent the rest of the day getting groceries from
a small group of stores not too far away. There was a
butcher shop, a general store, and—much to his delight—a bakery. He didn't know much about cooking,
but he was about to learn. He was famished, but he
didn't want to go out to a restaurant. He wanted to
spend as much time as he could in his new home finding
out about himself. At this moment he didn't want to
be around people.

Late in the evening, exhausted after his long day,

he fell across his bed only to awaken in the morning wondering where in the world he was. Then he remembered—he was home.

After washing up he started searching the house for clues that would bring him back to the present and perhaps help him regain the past. He began by going through every paper in his desk. Among the items was a letter from someone named Constance. It was dated many, many months ago, but it indicated to Lucas that he knew her quite well. At least it was a place to start.

Connie and her mother had been unpacking for what seemed days. Conrad was furious at the amount of money the two women had spent. Paris would never be the same again! It had tons of his money.

"Come look at my blue velvet, Father, please," she pleaded. "It's the very latest thing on the Continent." Somehow Connie had managed to pick up a slight English accent. It infuriated her father. All he needed was Connie being even more, well, Connie! She and Evelyn were driving him crazy. It had been so beautifully quiet for so long. His days of peace were at an end.

Picking up his hat, Conrad headed for the door.

"I'm going down to Tony's for a drink. Don't delay dinner for me."

"What?" Evelyn answered.

At that moment the knocker sounded and Conrad opened the door. There stood Lucas Forester.

"What the heck do you want?" Conrad asked. This

latest addition to his company he didn't need. It would only dredge up more problems.

"Pardon me, is this the residence of Constance Fillmore?"

"You trying to be smart, Lucas? What do you want, I asked. Give me an answer or get off of my porch!"

"I'm sorry, please forgive the intrusion, but I have a problem and I need to see a Constance Fillmore."

"You have a problem all right, boy, and right now it's me!"

"Who are you?" Lucas asked. He was not happy with the way this conversation was going.

"I'm her father, like you didn't know it, simpleton!"

"Please, may I come in? I think an explanation will help. Then if you don't like it, I'll gladly leave."

"Well, come in then, and, you louse, this had better be good!"

Conrad led Lucas back into the parlor, where the two women were still going through their new purchases. Connie was standing with her new blue velvet held in front of her. She looked up, saw Lucas, and turned white with surprise.

"My God, where did you come from?"

"Constance, you're swearing again!" Emily was ignoring the visitor.

"Please, if you will all bear with me. I do have an explanation for all of this."

"Well, let's hear it." Conrad sat heavily back in his chair.

"I was in San Francisco. There was an accident. It was only by chance that one of the volunteers at the hospital knew who I was. She was a friend of an aunt of mine, someone I cannot remember. I cannot remember anything, not even the accident. They say my memory will come back—it's driving me crazy. You cannot imagine what it is like to know nothing of your life. I had a key and only a few clues. At least I have come this far. I've found my home and I've found you. It's all I have.''

''Oh, Lucas, and I thought you had run away from me.'' Connie came forward, the blue dress forgotten, thrown carelessly to the floor. She put her arms around his neck and kissed him soundly. ''We were to be married, darling, and you just disappeared.''

Conrad stood like stone. Connie was at it again, her little game continued. She would marry Lucas yet, memory or no memory.

Conrad burst out laughing.

Just two days before, Jonathan Woodrow had come back into Hiram's life, two agonizing days of turmoil. His life had been turned upside down. Everything he had tried to hide for all these years had been thrown back in his face. There wasn't any use in denying the truth; although he had tried to bluff through the scene with Jonathan, it hadn't worked. There were too many people in Philadelphia who knew the truth. They would remember. It wouldn't matter now that he could make restitution, could explain, the time was long past when it would have sounded reasonable and honest. He had Agatha to think about; she had been the reason for his not making things right all those years ago. But who would believe him? No one. Especially the people at the bank in Philadelphia.

"You meet me Friday in the cemetery, the one west of town. Nobody ever goes there. I don't want to talk here, that Victor is too damned nosy, he might hear something. Wouldn't surprise me if the buzzard was listening at the door right now. You be there at exactly two o'clock, no later. You hear me, Hezekiah?"

He had spoken with clenched teeth, his face red, his eyes bulging. This was a man to be wary of. He was no fool. Hiram knew Jonathan wouldn't back down with any halfway promises. If he and Agatha and the bank were to survive this problem, Hiram would have to do whatever it was that Jonathan Woodrow wanted. There was no other way.

Nate had wondered just why Hiram wanted to ride into town alone that morning, but Hiram had explained he just thought the ride would do him good. He hadn't ridden a horse for too long a time anyway. It sounded like a reasonable excuse.

At one-thirty he left the bank and rode through the back streets of town, avoiding most of the townspeople that would normally be on the main street during the day. Jonathan was waiting.

"Took your time, didn't you?"

"Sorry." It was all that Hiram could say.

"Get off that mare and come over here. We can sit on this bench. We have a lot to talk about, Hezekiah. Time for restitution."

"What is it you want? I imagine it will do no good to explain what happened in Philadelphia."

"Explanations! You must be joking. You don't need to do any talking, you just listen, hear me?"

Hiram looked at Jonathan with disgust. He wished now he had simply brought a gun and shot this disgusting piece of dirt. That would have been the easy way out, but Hiram knew a man like this would have something somewhere that would come to light and destroy him in any case. Better to see what it was he wanted. He tried to believe there would be some way to salvage something of his life and Agatha's without ever revealing his past, but in his mind the struggle continued—and in his heart he knew that this man would take everything he could.

"I'm not going to turn you over to the authorities. Not if you cooperate with me. I don't give a hoot or a holler about the bank in Philadelphia. What the heck do I care? I was just a bank auditor, they paid me half what I should have gotten paid. I owe those cheapskates absolutely nothing! Or course, if we don't see eye to eye, I can always turn you in for a reward. I'm sure there's still some kind of reward on the books for you. Just remember that!"

Hiram looked down at the dry earth. He felt sick, his stomach was churning, his mouth was dry, and his heart was pounding. All he needed was another heart attack. This man would crucify Agatha, dear sweet Agatha who knew none of this.

"Well, Jonathan, what is it you want? Get it over with."

"Don't get a smart mouth with me, mister. After today we will be business associates in the finest sense of the word. You are going to take me in as a partner at the bank. My office will be next to your office, and half of everything you have at that bank will be in my name. You got that?''

''I can't do that! How in the world could I ever explain that to anyone! It just wouldn't work.''

''You better believe it will. Tell them that your precious daughter and I are engaged. Now that's not a bad idea. Don't look so stricken. I don't have to marry her, just tell people as your future son-in-law I should have a position at the bank. It doesn't have to happen tomorrow. I'll start coming out to the house. In a couple of weeks we can make the announcement. Once I'm settled in the bank your daughter can break the engagement. Now how's that sound, Hezekiah Bowman?''

Hiram was white as a sheet. He pulled out his medicine and quickly put a tablet under his tongue. This man was insane! But he knew that he had to comply with Jonathan's wishes. There was nothing else he could do!

Everyone at the dance seemed to be enjoying themselves. Constance looked beautiful in her soft blue gown, her hair piled high on her head, each bright curl moving as she and Lucas danced. He felt terribly uncomfortable. Everyone seemed to know him, and the confusion in his brain was multiplied over and over again as people would come up and greet him. He had asked that his problem not be revealed, and Constance had to keep whispering in his ear just who was who.

It was maddening. As for Connie herself, he could not imagine why he would have ever asked her to marry him. He didn't know what type of woman he would want for a wife, but this just did not feel right. Certainly not this artificially sweet, self-centered female. He wanted to become again what he had been before the accident, and since this was the only way to delve into the past, he had little choice but to continue seeing Constance. It was agonizing.

"Come, Lucas, let's get some punch." Her tone was very condescending. He felt as if he were being pulled by a ring in his nose.

"Constance, let's go home. My leg is bothering me again. I just can't dance any more."

"Oh, Lucas, you want us to be alone, don't you, sweet. What a nice thing to say."

"No, I just want to take you home and then go to my own home and get some rest."

Constance pouted all the way home in the hansom, and when Lucas didn't go inside with her, slammed the door in his face. In spite of his problems, Lucas had to laugh. It was a relief to be rid of her for the rest of the evening.

Home had begun to look familiar. At least it looked good to him each time he entered the house. He hadn't been able to find anything else of a business nature to assist in any new discoveries. Conrad had been very vacant in his answers to Lucas's questions, always telling him that once he felt a lot better he would tell him all that he knew. So far that had been absolutely nothing. Lucas had the vague impression that Conrad was holding something important back and had been pressing him to set a date for his wedding to Constance.

The night air felt wonderful after the warmth of the ballroom. Lucas was standing outside on his back porch looking out through the trees at the moonlight. It was a beautiful night. Across the fields came the sound of music, a tune Lucas was certain he had heard before. There it was again, that nagging feeling of what was so close to his grasp, but yet so far away. There was something and someone important that he should be remembering. It wouldn't come, it just lay dormant in the back of his brain. He pounded the porch railing with a clenched fist and swore. *Darn it, darn it, why can't I remember?*

Without knowing it at first, Lucas had come to a crossroads in his search. He realized, after standing in the night air for a long, long time, that he was going to have to search even harder in another direction. If Conrad wouldn't help him, maybe his housekeeper, once he found her, could. And the second thing on his mind became absolutely clear. He was not going to marry Constance Fillmore.

With a great deal of relief for having made this decision, he went back inside and slept. And he had a dream. It was about a dark-haired woman in a green satin gown.

Chapter Eleven

Hiram stood in the center of the parlor, his head bowed, his shoulders slumped. He seemed to shrink physically, suddenly old and worn far beyond his years. His eyes looked unseeing out the window, missing the distant mountains, the molded grace of the lower hillsides, and the blazing sunset, with its reds and golds throwing shadows that changed the landscape each moment as the day slowly ended.

Agatha stood across the room, her head tilted to one side, the rest of her body quiet. Her face was expressionless.

"There's something I must tell you. It's about a man named Jonathan Woodrow. He's someone from the past, someone who can destroy me, and you, and the bank.

"How can I tell you all that has happened? Where

can I begin? I can only pray you will understand and accept what I tell you. It started so long ago, a lifetime ago.''

He turned and looked at his daughter with pleading eyes. Agatha could only stare back, white faced, eyes wide, her face no longer placid. She was frightened and it showed clearly.

For a few moments neither spoke.

''Father, please, whatever it is, surely you can tell me, I'll understand. What has this man to do with us?''

Hiram turned again and stood looking out at the dying day.

''Please, Father, for God's sake, tell me! You're frightening me.''

Hiram still did not answer.

''Please, Father, no more silences, not now. There have been too many silences. I have always respected your privacy, but if this concerns both of us, you must tell me!''

Hiram's eyes filled with tears. He reached up and gruffly rubbed them away with the back of his hand. Finally he spoke.

''Please listen. Please try to understand. You may not, but please don't say anything until I am finished. The story isn't easy to tell, it was all so long ago that everything started. I'll try to bring it all back exactly as it was. It's all that I can do.''

Agatha sat down on her chair by the fireplace and waited.

Hiram continued to tell his secret.

''Your mother was dreadfully ill. I had tried every

doctor in Philadelphia and New York City. There was so little money and my salary as a bank teller was so small, so inadequate for what I was trying to do. She was dying, that beautiful flower of a woman. She was my life. A friend told me about a doctor in Europe that had had some success with her kind of illness. The cost of going was enormous, but I had to try to get the money somehow. I tried to borrow from the bank, friends, everyone, no one would listen. I realize now what I would not, could not accept then. She was dying, nothing could stop that. But I refused to believe it. So I did what I felt had to be done. First, I sent you to stay with friends in New York. Neither your mother nor I had any family and I wanted you away from Philadelphia, away where no one would think to look for you. Then late in the day I took the money I needed from the bank—embezzled, stole, call it what you will. It didn't matter to me what the consequences would be, I had to try and save her. All my plans were made, we would be leaving early the next day, a Saturday. The bank would not open until Monday morning, and by then she and I would be on a boat headed for England.''

He stopped talking, moved to his chair by the fireplace, sat down, and put his head in his hands. His whole body seemed to shiver despite the warm room. He began again to speak.

''The doctor was there when I arrived home. I knew by the look on his face that I had been too late. She was gone.

''I made arrangements for the funeral to be held

Sunday. It was her wish that it be done quickly, privately. The minister, the maid we had who had looked after your mother and you, and myself. No one else. It was over.

"Monday I left early for the bank. If I returned the money before the rest of the employees came in, no one would be the wiser. But when I went through the front door I was startled. A bank auditor was there going over the books. I went into the president's office and told him about your mother's death and asked for a few days off to settle things at home. He allowed this, of course."

Agatha moved from her chair and stood beside her father. She was pale and frightened. All of this was new to her, she had been too young to remember those very early years. Hiram reached up and gently held her hand for a moment, then relaxed his hold and slid farther back into the huge chair.

"Go on, I'm listening. What happened then?"

"The man who was auditing looked directly at me. I shall never forget that face, that look. I was certain he knew I had embezzled that money, but of course he could not have known, not yet. But there was no chance then to put the money back, no way to explain the theft, I would certainly have been sent to jail, and I still had you to think about.

"Please believe me, I had never even thought about doing anything dishonest before, nor since. But I was so desperate. And now I found myself in an impossible situation. Without even going home to pack, I dare not take that chance, I left immediately for New York to get you and take the next train out to anywhere.

"We finally got to San Francisco, and eventually here. I changed my name and of course yours. You know the rest."

They sat together for a few moments, each with their own thoughts, until Agatha spoke.

"I'm wondering what my real name is." And then she remembered.

"It's Bridie, isn't it?"

"Does it matter now? You have been Agatha Brunswick for all of your grown life. It could only hurt to think about it. Right now there's something else that has happened that is much more important than a name forgotten long ago.

"Over the years I had almost escaped the memories of those awful days. I thought that surely by now we were safe, free of the past. I was wrong."

Hiram leaned back in the chair and shut his eyes. The noise from the mantel clock sounded unnaturally loud. He raised a hand and rubbed it across his face and then held it to his chest before continuing.

"I should have known. If only I had tried to make amends, tried to return the money, it wasn't that much, just enough to get us started here. But I was afraid. Yes, a man like me—afraid! You were so little, your mother was gone, it was a time I would give anything to forget. It sounds so trite now to say I'm sorry. Desperation drove me to what I did, and once committed there was no turning back. Life's like that, you know. Once down a path, there can be no turning back.

Remorse is fine, but it changes nothing, absolutely nothing!

"And now the worst that could happen, what I have dreaded all these years, has happened. The auditor who looked so closely at my face . . . " Hiram hesitated a moment, then went on.

"He saw me, he remembered me. After all these years, he remembered me!"

Hiram stopped speaking for a moment. He seemed to slide further back within himself, to mold closer to the chair. The words he spoke next were difficult to say. Half-choking, he spit out the words, "He's Jonathan Woodrow! The man who saw me that day in the bank, the auditor who looked into my eyes, saw my face. He never forgot. He's here in town."

Agatha walked slowly to the window. Clouds were moving rapidly across the black night sky, making shadows that sulked across the back pasture. The bunkhouse and barn seemed to undulate, as if they had lives of their own. One of the horses whinnied, and the others could be heard moving around in their stalls. The whole world seemed restless tonight. The moon came out again from behind a cloud, bathing the world in a cold, ghostly gray. Agatha shivered.

"There's more, isn't there?"

Again Hiram was still.

"Isn't there?" Her voice was deep. It was almost a shout.

Agatha turned and looked at him.

"My God, yes. He wants to be a partner in the bank."

"How can you do that? What would everyone think? You wouldn't have a decent explanation for such an action."

Ashen, and now sweating profusely, Hiram seemed to wear his guilt like a garment. Now he revealed the rest.

"He can get control through you, by telling everyone that you are engaged to be married. God help me, that's what he wants to do."

Agatha could not answer. The room started spinning and the world turned black.

It was August now. Katie Monahan was busy with her dusting. It had been a long, hard day. The Culbertsons were nice people, but very untidy. It about had her ready to quit several times, but she needed the job. She wished her Mr. Luke would get back to town. There was nobody easier to work for than Mr. Luke.

Her work done, Katie was hanging up her apron when she overheard the cook talking to a friend as they sat huddled together at the kitchen table.

"I hear tell that Constance Fillmore's engagement to that fella, what's his name—oh, yes, Lucas something. Anyways, I hear tell it's on again!" She slammed her ample thigh with her hand, put her head back, and laughed—loud and long.

"You gotta be kiddin' me! On again? Do tell!" The cook's friend replied.

"Sure do! He got back from out west, been gone a long time. I hear tell he's been actin' kinda strange like. Don't think I'd want any part of a man acting strange. Not me, not likely!''

Katie interrupted. ''Mr. Lucas Forester is back in town? When? And how'd you hear about that?''

She wanted to know if she had heard right. Her Mr. Luke was back in town. Now why in God's green earth hadn't the man gotten in touch with her? They had always gotten along just fine.

''Heard from the Fillmore's cook, that's how! He's been back a month or so. Why, you thinkin' about goin' back to work for him? Seems if he wanted you, he'd a been in touch with you. Since he ain't, I wouldn't get too excited about it!''

The two women at the table laughed and exchanged knowing glances.

It was a long walk to Mr. Luke's, especially with the wind blowing and more thunder and lightning. A real summer storm. But at least it was driving away some of the heat. Katie kept on going in spite of her fears, and each time a clap of thunder would vibrate through the air, she would cringe and put her hands over her ears. It did little good.

At last the storm seemed to slow some and ahead she could see Mr. Luke's house. There was a light on in the library.

''Good. He must be home. Well, we shall see just why he doesn't want me cleaning for him anymore. He never had no complaint with me, so we will just find out!''

Lucas was busy going through every book on the shelves trying to find even a piece of paper to give him some kind of clue. What kind of clue he was seeking he didn't know, just something, anything!

There was a loud knock at the front door. Nobody had been to the house since his return, and the noise made him almost jump.

There stood a tiny, disheveled, wiry woman.

''Well, you gonna' stand there gawkin', or you gonna let me in?''

''Certainly, come on in.''

Katie pranced directly into the library as if she knew exactly where she wanted to go.

''Do I know you?'' he asked.

''What kind of a question is that? Do I know you? Do I know my own mother! Saints be praised! Mr. Luke, it's me, Katie. What in tarnation is the matter with you?''

With that Lucas grabbed the tiny woman and, lifting her off the floor, hugged her to his chest and danced around the room.

''I've found you, I've found you, I've found you!''

''Good grief, put me down! Have you gone crazy?''

A reception announcing the engagement of Mr. Jonathan Woodrow and Miss Agatha Brunswick was to be held at the King Mansion in early September. Agatha had refused to have one at home, much to Clarisa's relief. It was bad enough to see her mistress becoming engaged to that dreadful man, she wasn't about to cook for a crowd of gawking people, all of whom were aghast at such an obvious mismatch. It was the talk of Virginia City.

Nate and Clarisa were both walking around as if they were made of stone. Neither could speak about what was happening. Agatha didn't eat, wouldn't talk, just sat all day upstairs in her room, looking out the window. It was worse than before when Mr. Lucas hadn't come back.

"If this is a happy bride-to-be, I'm the Queen of Sheba!" Clarisa pronounced to an empty kitchen. She was busy making a pot of chicken soup. Maybe somebody would eat some of that. Mr. Brunswick was hardly ever at home, instead he was spending most of his time at the bank or off with that awful Jonathan Woodrow. It seemed that any excuse was good enough, anything to keep him away from the house and away from Agatha. Mr. Woodrow came out on Sundays for dinner and chattered while they all sat around the dining room table like a lot of dead people! Nobody answered except when they had to. At least that's what she told Nate, who had heard it again and again, but listened anyway. He and Clarisa had put off their wedding plans until things got better at Brunswick Manor, if indeed they ever did.

Clarisa was busy at the stove when Agatha walked into the room.

"We have to talk." Agatha had entered the room so silently that she startled Clarisa.

"Good God Almighty, you scared me witless!"

"I'm sorry, Clarisa. You have a cup of tea handy?"

"It will just take a second, the kettle's always hot."

They sat together at the kitchen table as they had so

many times before. Clarisa put her arm across the table and took Agatha's hand.

"You have something to tell me? I wish you would! I gotta know what's goin' on! It has Nate and me goin' in circles, we're that worried." She started to cry, she couldn't help herself.

"Oh, Clarisa, don't do that. You'll make me cry too!"

Agatha sighed and began.

"You have to trust me on this. There is a reason for all that has been happening. It has to be as it is, but no one must know what I am telling you, and it is only part of what's been happening. I cannot tell you everything. And it must not ever leave this room."

"Of course not!" Clarisa said indignantly. "You know me better than that; if you don't, you should!" Her voice was full of hurt and anger.

"I do, oh, I do. It's just that this is something far more important than anything else that has ever happened in this house, which is why part of it is just between my father and me. If and when he decides to, he can tell you the rest, the part I cannot tell you now. For now, can you be content with only a little of what has been going on?"

"Of course."

"And even this will leave a lot of questions. Just trust me, Clarisa. It is all I can do for now."

"Go on."

"I have become engaged to Jonathan Woodrow."

"Heck, I know that! It's what's been driving me mad!"

"You didn't let me finish."

"All right, finish."

"I shall never, and I promise you on the soul of my mother, I shall never marry him."

No one could work properly at the bank. They all tried, but the presence of Jonathan Woodrow made things unpleasant. The man did know his business; he was indeed a very fine accountant, but his behavior toward the employees left no doubt in anyone's mind that he was second in command. At times even that was in doubt. Hiram stayed in his office, arriving before anyone else, and no one saw much of him during the day. In spite of the doctor's advice, he stayed hours past closing. Everyone was worried, but no one dared mention it except to Victor, who had taken to staying completely away from either Hiram or Jonathan.

Marjorie walked into the somber establishment in time to catch Victor before he left for lunch.

"Hi, honey! How about treating a lady to lunch. There's a new Chinese place opened up just behind the Opera House. Want to try it, or do you have other plans?"

Victor was surprised to see his wife. She seldom came into the bank.

"One second. Let me get my hat."

As they were about to leave the bank, Jonathan came out of his new office and called to Victor.

"Victor! Just a moment."

He walked across the lobby and stood before them.

"And this would be Marjorie, your lovely wife.

Marjorie, I'm Jonathan Woodrow. This is indeed a pleasure. I've heard so many nice things about you.''

''And I have heard a good deal about you, Mr. Woodrow!'' Her tone was clear. Jonathan seemed not to notice.

''Going to lunch, are we? How nice. I was about to leave for a bite to eat myself.'' His words clearly implied that he would like to join them.

''That's nice. Good day, Mr. Woodrow.'' And with that Marjorie pranced sedately out of the bank. Victor could do nothing but follow.

Jonathan stood absolutely still.

''Ignore me, will you!'' he said quietly to himself. ''We will see about that!''

Chapter Twelve—September, 1875

Autumn had not yet arrived. The heat of summer held tightly to the early part of September. Clarisa, Nate, Lizbeth, and Agatha were busy setting up the reception with the help of two of Lizbeth's older boys. Inside King Mansion the heat was less oppressive than outside, but the mood was anything but joyous. Agatha only spoke to the others when it was absolutely necessary. She had lost a great deal of weight and her eyes looked heavy and red. Lizbeth kept up her usual chatter, which seemed to fill the void of silence that engulfed the gathering. She had brought the baby in his carriage, and Agatha kept a watch over Jacob, who was the center of attention.

Clarisa looked up at the ballroom ceiling with all of its streamers, then at the cluster of white bells that

hung over the reception table. She headed for the hallway, her head down, her hands up to her face.

''Now what's all that about?'' asked Lizbeth.

Agatha seemed not to notice; instead she was lifting
little Jacob out of his carriage and kissing his warm
neck. The baby giggled.

Lizbeth followed Clarisa out into the hallway and
back to the kitchen.

''What in the world is the matter with you, Clarisa?''

''I can't stand it! I just can't stand it! This whole
mess has to end. It feels like some kind of terrible
nightmare that just won't end! It must, it just must!''
She started to weep.

Lizbeth came and put her arms around her frail
friend. For once she said nothing, instead just held
Clarisa until the crying stopped.

''She's our friend, our dear friend. All we can do,
Clarisa, is stay by her side and help all we can.''

''Oh, how I wish Mr. Lucas would come back. If
only I could see him for a few minutes, I'm sure I
could fix things right again. But we can't find him!''

''You mean to tell me you tried to find him? When?
Where? Does Agatha know?''

''Shush, she'll hear you clear back there. No, she
doesn't know, and don't you dare tell her! You hear
me?''

Nate was calling for them from the hallway.

''Nate went to San Francisco. He tried everything.
The man's just fallen off the earth. I know somethin'
awful has happened to him. He would never have left

Agatha like this. He loved her, I could tell. It was plain as anything."

"You two comin' back in here? I gotta get some more womanly advice about where to put these here chairs!" Nate was making himself heard all the way down the hall.

Agatha was holding Jacob and looking down into his tiny pink face. "I won't ever have any sweet babies like this." She spoke directly to the soft bundle who smelled like powder and felt soft as a rose petal. She put the baby back into his carriage and continued helping to decorate the room.

The reception was to be held the following week, the day after the new musical at Piper's Opera House. She wondered, not for the first time, just how she would ever get through such a farce.

Katie didn't pretend that she understood anybody losing their memory. How was such a thing possible? Mr. Lucas had been asking her all kinds of questions, and she had tried to tell him everything she knew, which wasn't much.

"You never were much of a man to keep papers around. You got a couple of other businesspeople you associate with—Mr. Fillmore is the only name comes to mind. If I can think of anyone else I will, but it just ain't there right now!" Her irritation was directed more at herself than at Lucas.

"One thing I do remember, you gave a box of papers for safekeeping to somebody last time you had a meeting."

"Who did I give the papers to, can you remember that?"

"Seems like it was that Mr. Fillmore. Big man, white hair, that him?"

"That's him—I'm certain. Anything else?"

"Like I said, if I remember a single, solitary thing I'll come right out with it."

Lucas was furious. He knew Conrad was not telling him what he desperately needed to know. But he could not push the man; then he would never find out anything. And there was Connie. What in the world was he going to do about Connie? His mind kept going in wild directions. Every once in a while some image would flash though his brain, then disappear. The more he tried, the less he knew.

It was just after lunch that Katie left and Lucas was tired. Tired of thinking, of searching, of looking. His head hurt. He pulled a book down from the shelf in the library and sat in his comfortable, now familiar, chair to read. In seconds he was asleep.

"Piper's Opera House is proud to present Miss Lillie Langtry in a premier performance." Clarisa had read the notice while in town with Nate buying groceries. Jonathan insisted that he and Agatha go together. Nothing would please him more, nothing would please her less. It was all she could do just to be civil to the man. Another farce, another evening with a man she despised.

The auditorium was filled to capacity. Jonathan had reserved a box and had invited Hiram, Dr. Jake, Victor, and Marjorie to attend. When they heard who was performing, they all accepted. At least having such a celebrity in their midst helped sustain them in the company of a host they all detested. It was becoming more and more difficult to be pleasant to Jonathan, even for Agatha's sake. Only Hiram knew the truth and the truth was bitter gall.

Music was already coming from the orchestra pit as Jonathan and Agatha arrived to join their guests waiting in the lobby. He had gotten to Brunswick Manor late, smiling and apologetic. He smelled of whiskey.

The first half of the program was over and the house lights were turned up. They were garishly bright. Most of the audience knew exactly who was in the box closest to the stage. Tittering could be heard from behind the fans held by the well-dressed ladies in the audience, and conversation among the men perspiring in the dreadful heat of the stuffy auditorium. Everyone knew of the engagement and of Jonathan's recent addition as vice president at the bank. It was the main topic of conversation all over Virginia City.

"My dear," Jonathan spoke, "I have something to give you. I was going to wait until tomorrow evening, but this seems like a much better time. You will be so busy at the reception, and of course, so will I."

Jonathan reached into his side pocket, pulled out a jewelry box, opened it, and in front of everyone in the audience, lifted Agatha's hand and placed a diamond ring on her finger. Agatha turned white. Until this second she had reasoned that somehow this horror would end, Lucas would return, everything her father had told her would be a lie. It was not to be. She forced a wan smile from her lips and vowed to herself that never, ever, would this man become her husband.

Leaning forward, he whispered into her ear, "I don't care what your father thinks, you and I will be married. You can count on it, pretty lady!"

"You promised him!" she replied, her words bitter, her hands rigid in his grasp.

"I never kept a promise in my life. But you will marry me, dear heart—or the world will know exactly who you are and your precious, safe world will come tumbling down. Just remember that!"

Lucas was dreaming. He was in a boat, and the water around it was rough with white-capped waves that crashed over the top of the vessel. Ahead of him he could see a woman standing at the rail. Seawater was running down her face, and her clothes were soaking wet. She was trying to hold on to the railing but the wind was too strong and she was losing her grip. He tried to walk toward her, but his feet kept slipping and his movements were torture. Over and over again he tried going forward, but somehow she kept getting farther and farther away from him. He watched in horror as a huge wave swept over the boat and she was gone.

"Agatha!" he screamed, awake and soaked with sweat. "I said 'Agatha!' My God, I said 'Agatha'! Who is Agatha?"

* * *

Agatha's friends were pleasant to her at the reception. Most, if not all, were puzzled that she would be marrying a man like Jonathan. He was anything but handsome and had a manner that irritated almost everyone he met. The others, business associates of Hiram's and people from town, were less inclined. The same behavior Victor had seen at the Opera House was in blatant evidence. Marjorie was furious! Agatha seemed not to notice and walked around with a pasted smile on her face.

"She has to be numb! Just what in the world is happening, Victor? You're at that bank all day long! Don't you ever hear anything?"

"No." It was all he could say.

"Men! You make me sick. I cannot imagine that beautiful, sweet, kind, gentle woman married to that obnoxious man! I won't even call him a man. And a gentleman! Ha!" She spit out the last word.

"There's only one thing I wonder about." Victor was speaking. Marjorie was close beside him in an instant.

"What!"

"I heard them speaking once. I didn't mean to eavesdrop, but Jonathan was saying something about Philadelphia. We don't do any business with anybody from Philadelphia! I don't have even a notion of what it could mean. It must mean something. But it isn't bad enough that Agatha is involved with the man. You should see what it is doing to Hiram! I don't know how he handles the tension at the bank—not with his heart problems."

Their conversation stopped when Agatha asked for quiet.

"I have an announcement to make!"

The room waited, expecting to hear that a date for the upcoming nuptials would be announced. Instead she continued, "It is with deep pleasure that I wish to announce another engagement. My dearest friends, Clarisa Moore and Nathan Culpepper, are going to be married in the near future. I thought this would be a good time to tell all of their friends."

There was a sudden rush of people toward Clarisa and Nate, who were standing at the door. Everyone applauded, Clarisa turned bright red, and Nate's smile seemed to cover his entire face. The look Clarisa sent Agatha's way seemed to say, I'll get you for this! She was embarrassed. If the reception hadn't been for Agatha and Jonathan, she would have been a happy woman. As it was, Clarisa could not forget why they were here. And again she wondered just where Lucas Forester was.

Bits and pieces of memory were returning. Faces mostly, but a few scattered portions of his life before the accident were giving him, at last, some solid footing. He could remember his Aunt Bea. He could see clearly the room with a fireplace upstairs and the view from the window. At times he would remember his brother's face, and then it would fall into shadow, the features blurred, then nothing again. But it was something. And then there was Agatha. Katie didn't know anything about any Agatha. Lucas couldn't push his mind any further than it would go. Every time he tried he would get a tremendous headache and sweaty palms. But there was one thing he knew he could do. He was going to confront Conrad and find out where his papers were.

Music and the sound of muffled voices were coming through the open parlor window as he rode up to the Fillmore house. For the first time he noticed the huge brass knocker, the tubs of marigolds still in bloom, and the color of the iron mud scrapper by the door. It had started to rust. He couldn't imagine why he noticed such a thing, but little things became more and more important as Lucas began to have some hope of his life returning to—to what? He still did not know.

Florence came to the door flushed and angry looking, as always. He would be glad when he was done with whatever it was that affected him so deeply, this thing he felt had been hidden from him by these people. A deepening anger came to the surface. Lost memory or not, he did not like these people. He wondered if he ever had.

"Is Conrad in?"

"Come in, Mr. Forester, I'm sure he will see you. Do you wish to see Miss Connie, also? She's upstairs resting."

"Not just now. First Mr. Fillmore. I'll let you know about Miss Constance."

Lucas waited in the library. He searched the shelves, looking for titles that might match the kind of books he had at home. There were none. Most of the covers looked untouched. He lifted down a book of poems;

its cover was intact. He put the book down on a desk
when he heard Conrad coming into the room.

"My boy, it is good to see you. Remembering anything yet?" There was a look of amusement in his eyes
and a half smile showing at the corners of his mouth.

"Some things. My Aunt Bea for one. I wonder why
you didn't tell me about her? Was it some kind of
secret?"

Conrad moved across the room to grab Lucas by his
shoulders before he spoke.

"Now, now. It's just that Mother and Connie and I
felt it would be better if things came to you without
our interfering. Come, sit down. Would you like a
glass of sherry?"

Something in Conrad's condescending tone infuriated Lucas.

"No, I don't want a darned glass of sherry. I want
some answers. And I want the papers I left with you!
How long did you intend keeping them? Or was that
too part of your plan to keep me in the dark until my
memory came back?" Lucas stood in the center of the
room, his fists clenched. He did not know just where
all this anger had come from, and he could not contain
it, could not even try.

"My boy, my boy, what ever do you mean? There's
no use being this angry about such a small matter. I
had forgotten all about your papers. Wait right here,
I'll get them for you."

Conrad moved out of the room. He hadn't had time
to go through the papers Lucas had left. Most of them
were for Lucas's accountant who had long since used

them to audit his books along with Conrad's. What else the box contained he had no idea. It wouldn't do to keep it anyway, not in the mood Lucas was in just now. The box was in the hall closet under the stairs. It took him a few moments to retrieve it, and as he moved back through the foyer he saw Connie coming down the stairs.

"What's all the commotion? I could hear shouting all the way upstairs. It was disturbing. I did so need a rest."

"It's Lucas. I'm giving him back some papers."

"Oh, Lucas. I want to see him."

Conrad put the box down and walked to his daughter. He spoke in a low voice so that Lucas, not too far away, would not hear.

"If you are going to marry the lad, you'd better be quick about it. His memory is coming back. Just a little, but you cannot tell. It's now, or never, dear girl!"

Constance looked startled. She squared her shoulders, tossed her tiny curls, and followed her father into the library.

"Lucas, darling, why didn't you have Florence wake me? I am so glad to see you, we have to talk just as soon as you and father are finished. Mother is getting anxious about our wedding plans."

Her tiny mouth was pouting as she put her arms around his neck. Lucas pulled her arms down to her sides; his fury had only increased. He couldn't seem to even stand her touch.

"And that's another thing. I don't remember anything about any wedding plans. There is no engagement, nothing. As far as I can tell you right now, you and I are not ever going to be married. I cannot imagine that I ever harbored any such idea. There's nothing between us, Connie, I cannot believe there ever was!''

''You jerk!'' Conrad was furious. He grabbed Lucas by the throat and slammed him against the wall. ''Not again, you cannot hurt Constance again!''

Lucas smiled. He could not help himself.

''So I had broken an engagement once before, did I?'' He laughed out loud.

Constance stood, credulous, as her father swung a heavy fist and smashed the laughing Lucas across his face. He fell heavily to the floor. Then, rising, he started toward Conrad, but stopped abruptly.

''You're not worth it.''

''Lucas, you cannot leave me? What will I tell people? Not again, it will be too embarrassing.''

''That's too bad, isn't it—and whose fault is all of this, Constance? Mine? Not in a million years. You've brought on this embarrassment, as you call it, yourself! I no longer give a damn!''

With those few words he picked up the box of papers and walked out of the room. Suddenly he turned and spoke again to Conrad, who stood in the center of the room, his face red with anger, his white hair disheveled.

Constance started to pick up the book of poems Lucas had left on the desk, but Conrad grabbed her wrist before she could toss it across the room.

''I'm going back to Virginia City, to Agatha!''

Only after the words were spoken did he realize what he had just said.

He was smiling as he walked away from the house in Kansas City. The box in his arms was heavy and his limp more pronounced as he moved down the steps, but he didn't care!

He was remembering a lovely face.

Agatha's face.

Chapter Thirteen

A crescent moon was just beginning its journey through the night sky as Lucas stepped off the train at Carson City. It would be morning before he could continue on to Virginia City. Too much time had passed for him to depend on a letter to Agatha, his explanation must come in person, not on any written page which could never convey his feelings. The need to see her again was so strong he wanted to walk all the way up the mountain without waiting, but morning would have to do.

People were moving around the city as people always do; a group of children were still playing tag in the park, now heavy with the shadows of early evening. Two businessmen, carrying their luggage, were crossing the street heading for the Ormsby House, and a lumbering wagon, the driver in no hurry, was turning off the main street going west.

He was suddenly very hungry. He couldn't remember when he had eaten last. Beside the park was a small restaurant whose lights had just been turned on. It looked pleasant enough and Lucas walked past the children, now playing in almost total darkness, across the street and into "Ye Olde Carson Cafe." On the way to his table he noticed a copy of the *Territorial Enterprise*, the Virginia City newspaper. He picked it up to read while he ate.

Lucas ordered the blue plate special and coffee, but when the waitress arrived with his food, her customer was gone. Lucas was standing outside leaning heavily on the side of the building. He had just read this announcement: "Mr. Hiram Brunswick announces the engagement of his daughter, Miss Agatha Brunswick, to Mr. Jonathan Woodrow."

Nate gave Clarisa a gentle poke on her arm with his elbow, trying to make her laugh, or at least smile. They had been sitting in St. Paul's Episcopal Church, on the last pew, waiting for the pastor to come over from the rectory. They were early, he was late.

"This place is sure beautiful," Nate said as he looked around the church, noticing the hand hewn pine beams, the beautiful pipe organ.

"Are you happy, sweet cake?"

Clarisa turned her head and looked at Nate.

"Sweet cake! Ha!" But she was smiling. "I

wouldn't be doin' this except for Agatha. We should've waited. But this is what she wants. So be it!''

"You mean to tell me, woman, you ain't anxious as me to get hitched?'' Nate pretended to look injured.

"No, you danged fool! I just can't think straight. Things are comin' up worse and worse at home. You see how bad Mr. Brunswick looks lately?''

The two sat holding hands, looking out through the stained-glass windows, the smell of candles and wood like a pleasant perfume filling the church.

"I wonder why he don't do somethin' about what's goin' on in our lives?''

"Who?" Asked Nate.

"God,'' she answered.

That evening, with only Agatha and Hiram present, Clarisa and Nate became man and wife. Clarisa had her way. There was no big wedding, just three people that she loved with her—Agatha, Mr. Brunswick, and her Nate.

Lizbeth was as excited as a woman could be. She was actually going to Sacramento to visit her sister who would be seeing the new baby for the first time. John had time off from the mine and offered to take care of the house.

"You just take Jacob, I'll take care of the rest of the children. It's about time you got away from that house.''

The train station was jammed with people heading for Sacramento or San Francisco. Lizbeth thought it was just wonderful and was flushed with excitement.

"Just think, Agatha, I am actually going to take a train to Sacramento! Will you do me a favor and look in on John and the children? You know how he is, nothing will be done right. Anyway, Jacob will get to see his aunt, and I will get to see her family. It's been years, just years!"

"Lizbeth, do you ever, ever slow down?" Agatha laughed.

"Oh, you know me, always busy, always loud and mouthy. I just can't help it. John says the only time I'm quiet is when I'm asleep!"

Agatha helped Lizbeth up the stairs, and the conductor took Jacob all wrapped snug in a warm blanket. He was sound asleep.

"You have fun, now, you hear me?" Agatha stepped back and as the train pulled out of the station she waved at Lizbeth and stood watching as her friend moved out of sight. Only then did she turn to leave the station.

As the last car pulled past the platform, Lucas looked out just in time to see Agatha as she turned her back to the train.

Hours later the train had stopped in Sacramento. Lucas left his seat to walk outside. He watched as Lizbeth stepped down from the coach with Jacob. He had to speak to her. Taking out a small notebook, he wrote down his name and Mildred's address in San Francisco.

"Pardon me, you're a friend of Agatha Brunswick, aren't you?"

"Sir, do I know you?"

"No, but I'm Lucas Forester, and you?"

"Lucas Forester! I'll be darned! Pardon my swearing, but have you any idea how many people have been looking for you? Agatha just about went crazy! Oh, my God, I forgot. She's engaged to somebody else! Oh, I am sorry."

"It's all right, I know. Would you be Lizbeth? Agatha told me so much about you. How is Agatha?"

"Miserable, I just cannot imagine why she is going to marry that man, nobody does, it is just awful. But I just have to mind my own business and keep my mouth shut."

"Will you do something for me, Lizbeth? Please? I want you to keep my address, but you are not to tell anyone where I am. I just want someone in Virginia City to have it in case Agatha ever needs me."

Just as the train was about to start again, Lizbeth's sister came rushing up to them, hair flying in all directions, and children straggling along behind.

Lucas walked quickly to the train and stepped into the coach. Lizbeth turned to see him and shouted at him as the train started moving down the tracks:

"Lucas, wait! Wait!"

It wasn't any use, her voice could scarcely be heard over the sound of the train whistle. He was gone.

"I didn't get to tell him," she said to her sister, who was standing there with a questioning look on her face.

"Tell who, what?"

"Tell Lucas Forester that Agatha Brunswick loves him like crazy, that's what!"

*   *   *

Knickerbocker Engine Co., No. 5, was having a dance. Everyone was there including all the members of Engine Co., No. 6, and the Hand-in-Hand Hose Co., No. 1. Jonathan had insisted that Agatha accompany him; Clarisa and Nate followed, Hiram declined. He had been feeling poorly and was staying home. At Agatha's suggestions Jake went up the hill to Brunswick Manor, ostensibly to play chess with Hiram. He was in fact taking the time to look over his good friend, who had canceled his last two doctor's appointments.

The dance was going very well; everyone seemed to be having a great time. Lizbeth saw Clarisa watching from the sidelines.

"Have you seen Agatha?" she asked.

Clarisa replied, "She's over there with Mrs. Graves. Why?"

"You will have to trust me on this. And you must give me your word you will not ask any questions, or repeat anything I tell you to a soul."

"Yes, I promise. What the devil are you talkin' about, Lizbeth?"

"Just this. If there is any trouble, outside of what's currently happening, with Agatha, you are to tell me directly, and I do mean directly. You send Nate to me if the least little thing happens. I will need to know right away." Her lips were tight, and she was squinting her eyes almost shut as if to emphasize what she was saying.

"I don't know what you're up to, Lizbeth, but you know danged well I tell you everything about our Agatha! Straight-a-ways every time? What in tarnation is the matter with you, gal?''

Again she tightened her lips into a thin line.

''That's all I can say. You just believe me, it's important, as important as anything ever was. Anything happens, I've just got to know.''

Later Clarisa puzzled over what Lizbeth had said. None of it made sense, but most of the time Lizbeth didn't make sense anyway. But much later she would remember their conversation.

The room had turned chilly in spite of the warmth from the fireplace. Jake saw that the fire was down to small embers and rose to put on an extra log.

''It's cold in here, Hiram. You feeling all right?''

''I'm fine . . . well, as much as can be expected for a man who has had a heart attack. Don't expect I should feel any better.''

''You look terrible! You're driving yourself too hard at that bank, you neglect yourself, you don't listen to my orders, your complexion is gray. Sure you feel great! Darn you, Hiram, your daughter needs you, I need you, we all need you! What in heaven's name are you trying to do, kill yourself?''

Hiram sighed. ''I know. You just don't understand. There are some things about me you don't know. I've started down a path and I can't turn away. It's out of my control. It's tearing me apart, Agatha apart, and I can't do a thing about it!'' He buried his head in his hands.

Jake turned and warmed his hands over the fire. The chessboard sat untouched on the library table.

"Hiram, I'm your best friend. You can tell me anything, if it will help. Isn't there something I can do? You know I'll do anything for you and Agatha. Hell, there must be a solution to whatever this problem is!"

"I'm sorry, Jake. This is a burden I will have to carry alone. If the time ever comes that I can divulge anything, you will be the first one to know."

Off in the distance, the sound of laughter and music from the dance could be heard drifting across the valley, and up in the mountains the wild horses moved restlessly among the cactus and sage. The moon was high in the sky, the stars were diamonds—and below, the world of Hiram Brunswick was crashing down around him.

"One thing is certain: there is something terribly wrong." Hiram looked toward his friend, his eyes pleading that he ask no questions.

"I know, I know! You can't tell me. That's not important right now. What is important is that you know something. Should something ever happen to you I will see that Agatha, Clarisa, Nate, and the ranch are taken care of. I love them like my own family, all of them including you. Remember that always! Always! Do you hear me?"

Hiram was looking directly at Jake. He rose and moved across the room to his friend and embraced him. Tears were streaming down his face.

"My dear friend, how can I ever thank you? I have

done nothing to deserve a friend like you. God bless you, Jake.''

"Just let me know, when you can, what it is that is tearing this family apart—when you can, Hiram. I'm not trying to push you. I am only here to help."

A new vein of gold had been found near Gold City. The assay office was busier than it had ever been, and the banks in town were feeling the upsurge in business. Virginia Bank was no different than the rest, and Victor hadn't had time to even speak to Hiram all morning. It was time for lunch but he didn't see how he would even manage a half an hour away from his desk.

"Jimmy, would you come over here, please?" He was speaking to one of his newer tellers.

"Yes, sir, what can I do for you?"

"Do you think you could go out and get me a sandwich? I'm not going to be able to leave the bank for lunch."

"Sure can. I was about to go anyway. What do you want?"

That settled, Victor moved back to his office and shut the door. Paperwork was piled everywhere on his desk. He had been trying to catch up on his work and it wasn't helping that Hiram was adding even more to his overworked clerk.

"When will this whole mess end?" He spoke to no one. Out of the window he could see Jonathan, dressed like a dandy, walking down toward the center of town.

"I'll bet he has a nice, long lunch!" He slammed

his fist down on the desk and papers scattered everywhere.

"That certainly helped!" Standing, he moved around picking up the assortment of loan papers, correspondence, and some notes from Hiram he hadn't had a moment to look at for days.

He let out a long sigh of frustration. He was a man almost at the end of his patience.

At six that evening everyone but Hiram and Jonathan had left the building—Hiram because he hated going home, Jonathan because he wanted to speak to Hiram. There were papers to be signed that couldn't wait any longer. He wondered how the bank president would feel when he read what was in the agreement. It wouldn't matter that he didn't like what it said. Hiram would have no choice but to sign.

"Hiram, you busy?"

"You have the door open, I guess that means you want to come in, so come in. And shut it behind you."

"No reason to be nasty. There's no reason we can't be friends. You keep taking all of this too seriously."

"How in the world would you expect me to take all of this? You come into my life and my daughter's and all but destroy us. Am I supposed to like it? You're a danged fool if you think so."

Hiram rose from his chair and walked to the window, his back to Jonathan. The pain in his chest never went away these days, and at this moment it was increasing, as it always did at the sight of Jonathan.

"We have to get a few things straightened out,

Hiram. For one thing, there's to be an increase in my stock.''

"A what?'' Hiram turned and almost screamed his answer. "You must really be crazy!''

"Since you're the largest stockholder in the company, it shouldn't be any problem. Just turn some of it over to me. Here, I have the papers all ready.'' He shoved them across the desk at Hiram, who sat down heavily in his chair.

"You really don't have much choice, dear chap. Here's a pen.'' His eyes were cold and threatening.

"Sign them!'' He forced a pen in Hiram's hand. He was gritting his teeth together in a defiant grimace.

Hiram's hand shook, his face was burning fire red, his heart was racing, and the pain was unbearable. He signed the document.

Jonathan looked down at the paper. Over the top he could see the container of Hiram's medication. Hiram was clutching his chest with one hand, the other was groping for the pills, his face now ashen.

"Give me, give me . . . '' The sentence was never finished. Jonathan reached over and picked up the box. Hiram stared at him, horrified.

"Please, in the name of God!''

Jonathan watched as Hiram leaned heavily across the desk. The inkwell splattered to the floor sending a black stain cascading across the floor. Hiram looked one more time toward Jonathan, then his eyes rolled back in his head and he slumped to the floor. Jonathan did nothing for a minute; he simply watched as Hiram's breathing stopped. The man was dead when Jonathan leaned down and placed the medicine box into Hiram's pocket, walked out of the office and into his own, picked up his hat, and went out the front door and back to Mrs. Hoffman's boardinghouse.

The rain had finally stopped. Agatha saw a rainbow out of the corner of her eye and turned to see all of its luminous colors shimmering in the sun. The others had left the cemetery; only Clarisa and Nate stood waiting at the top of the hill. Agatha had refused to leave until Hiram's grave had been covered over. There were flowers everywhere.

"Dear lady, you cannot stand here all day!" Jonathan was impatient.

"Just stay away from me!"

Jonathan stood beside her, not moving.

"Get away from me. Now!"

"We'll talk about things later—when you are feeling better. I'll be at Mrs. Hoffman's if you need me."

"I won't ever need you. Now get out of my sight!"

"You shouldn't speak to me in that tone, Agatha. But I can excuse you, under the circumstances. I'll be over to the house sometime next week."

Agatha did not answer, but stood staring off across the cemetery, waiting for Jonathan to leave. He left just as Jake came riding up in his buggy. Jake got out and hurried down to stand beside her. He took her hand and held it tightly.

"I couldn't get here. There's been an accident in one of the mines. Nobody killed, thank God, but a lot of injuries. It's all right now, but I couldn't leave. Darn it, I couldn't leave.''

He put his arm around Agatha.

''Who will you play chess with now?'' she questioned.

He hugged her gently. ''I don't know, I just don't know. There will never be another Hiram, never. People loved him—you know that, don't you?''

Taking her hand, he led her slowly toward Clarisa and Nate.

''Did you know how many people he's helped in this town, how much of his own money he gave to people who needed it? He never asked a thing in return. He just wanted to live quietly at the manor, ride his horse up into the hills, play chess, and be himself. It's all he ever asked of life. He was too young to die.''

They were close to the top of the rise.

''I tried to tell him to take it easy. Something was driving him, causing him tremendous pain. It's what killed him. You know that, don't you, Agatha?''

''Yes, I know.''

''If you need to talk about it, you know I'm here. I tried to get him to tell me what it was that was tearing him apart. He wouldn't, or he couldn't. I never figured out which one. Please, Agatha, if you need anything just let me know, and I'll be there. I told him that I would take care of you, Clarisa, Nate, and the ranch should this happen.''

''Thank you, Jake. There is a lot I need to take care of, I know that. I know things you don't know. It will just take a little time. Your caring—it means so much.

But don't worry, it will all be over soon. I have so much to do. In the meantime, if I need you I promise to get in touch. Don't worry about me. Things will be fine.''

She seemed so sure of her self and this puzzled Jake, but then he remembered that she was Hiram Brunswick's daughter.

They parted at the top of the hill; Jake went to take care of his patients at the hospital and Agatha went home to decide exactly how to go on with her own life. She had to handle the problems she had with the bank and most of all with Jonathan Woodrow.

Lizbeth was preparing her husband's lunch. He would be down in the mine a long time today. The new vein was a good one and everyone was busy. It was difficult for her to keep her mind on John and the children; she kept remembering what Lucas had said at the train station in Sacramento. Hiram's death was a tragedy that Agatha would learn, in time, to accept. But this wasn't trouble in the usual sense. It wasn't what Lucas meant. It would be best to wait until she knew exactly what Agatha would be doing about Jonathan Woodrow. Until then, she knew it was best to be quiet about the meeting with Lucas, but it was difficult for her to keep her promise.

"Here's your lunch kettle, John. You take care of yourself. I'll see you this evening. I'm going to take the children for a picnic with Agatha. We'll be up the hill behind the manor." John smiled. "It's kinda windy for a picnic, don't you think?"

"I know, but Agatha needs company and the children and I need to get out of the house. Now you just go on to work and leave me be!''

John kissed her cheek and left for work.

The date was September 26, 1875.

Jacob was being an angel today, Agatha thought. He had always been a good baby, but today he cooed and smiled and slept. She, Lizbeth, Clarisa, and the children were having their picnic under the cottonwoods on the hill beyond the manor. The little ones were having a wonderful time riding a donkey and climbing in one of the trees.

"You be careful!" Lizbeth scolded. "I don't need anybody breaking an arm!"

Agatha was smiling. Clarisa watched her friend and felt good about how she looked. For the first time since her father's death, she had a little color in her cheeks.

"Mama, look over there at that smoke. It looks like a house is on fire.'' One of the older children was pointing toward town.

"Matthew, behave yourself. Go help your sister get down from that tree!"

"But Mama, look!"

Agatha and Clarisa stood up and looked toward town. Just then the sound of a firehouse bell sounded and the smoke changed to flames.

"My God, my house!" Lizbeth screamed. The fire, whipped by the strong winds, had already traveled down the street toward her home.

Firehouse bells were ringing from all of the fire companies. Screaming people, horses, and other animals were all running through the smoke-filled streets in panic. Everywhere there was chaos. The tinder-dry houses, just behind the opera house, were already burning. The fire was almost to the bank.

Lizbeth's children gathered around her, clutching her skirts. Jacob began to cry.

The bank's board of directors was to meet in a week, and Jonathan hadn't let the documents giving him control of the bank out of his sight for one minute. He was thinking about just what he would say at the meeting. He knew for certain the reactions of the others involved. There wasn't a thing they could do about it. Leaning back in his chair, he smiled.

Outside, in his teller's booth, Jimmy was busy counting change. He was two cents short and was determined to find his error. It was stuffy in the bank, or he was just nervous—it was hard not to be these days with Mr. Woodrow taking charge. Going to the window at the front of the lobby, he opened it to let in a little air. It was then that he saw the smoke. Some fool burning trash again. He returned to his teller cage.

"It smells funny in here." Victor had just entered the lobby from his office. He walked to the front door and looked outside.

"My God, there's a fire, it's just up the street. Everybody lock your drawers, get out of here."

No one moved.

"Do as I say, get out of here!"

The sound of fire bells and horses suddenly shattered the silence. The sound of people running screaming through the streets, animals in panic, and fire bells could all be heard clearly from inside the bank.

Jonathan came out of his office, his face white with fear. "My God, the town's on fire, I've got to get out!"

"Everybody, get out! I mean it, get out, now!" It was Victor who spoke, concern filling his voice.

Everybody did except Victor, who ran back into his office to retrieve the bank ledgers.

Jonathan felt inside his coat pocket to be certain the documents that Hiram had signed were still there. But the money, the vault was filled with money! If the fire got too hot the money would be destroyed. Rushing into the vault, he started grabbing bundles and stuffing them into a canvas bag. His back was to the door.

Victor came out of his office and did what he had done at the end of every day of his employ at the bank. He ran to the vault and slammed the door shut and spun the lock closed.

The darkness was complete. And the sound of Jonathan's screams bounced off the solid walls like an echo in an empty cave.

No one could hear him, no one in the world!

Chapter Fourteen—October 1875

Any plans Clarisa and Nate had were, for the present, put aside. They would stay at the manor to be near Agatha until some future time. Too much had happened too quickly to leave Agatha alone. They had always been there when she needed them. Now would be no different.

Nate had seen that the last cutting of alfalfa was bailed, the horse barn repaired, and the property put in proper order. Clarisa had taken care of the manor and done everything she could to make things easier for Agatha.

Ike Masterly made arrangements to buy the ranch, all but the agreed-upon ten acres, the manor, and the horse barn. The price had been exactly as first set, and it was with great relief to Agatha that the property had been sold. The sale was being handled through the family attorney, along with the usual probate of Hiram's estate. The board of trustees, with Victor's help, were taking care of the bank for the present. It was all being done quietly, without too much stress on Agatha.

Agatha started to ride her mare Jubilee each morning and was eating properly again, but was still too quiet. She refused any kind of social invitation. She seldom even visited Lizbeth.

She would stand and look off into the hills, watching the changing skies, the deepening shadows. Sometimes at night Clarisa and Nate would hear her moving around her room, pacing back and forth between her bed and the window that overlooked town. She seemed to be waiting, waiting.

Morning would always come again, the same each day. There was very little change and less company, until one afternoon when Lizbeth came riding into the yard in an old buckboard.

"Is Agatha around?"

"No, Lizbeth, she's up in the hills somewhere, riding. Why?"

"I thought so. I didn't want her around when I gave you this. It's Lucas's address in San Francisco."

Clarisa's mouth flew open.

"Where did you get this?"

"I met him at the train station in Sacramento. He looked awful; he has a limp and there are some scars on his forehead. Looks like he's been in some kind of accident. There wasn't time to find out! He just gave me this and said to write to him if anything happened to Agatha, should she need him, or anything."

"Why didn't you tell me before? That's been ages ago!"

" 'Cause he made me promise not to. He knew she was engaged to Jonathan. I opened my big mouth, but I could tell he already knew."

"My God! Oh, Lizbeth, don't tell her! Promise me you won't!"

"I hadn't planned to, I just thought that you and Nate should know, you would know what to do. I sure don't! I don't want to see her hurt any more, neither do you. Do you think we should get in touch with him?" She kept on talking and followed Clarisa as she rushed outside toward the barn to find Nate.

"Good Lord, woman, what's goin' on?"

"Here, you just look at this." Clarisa handed him the piece of paper.

"Don't just stand there, you sit yourself down and write something—I'll send a telegram, send it to him right now! I'll take it into town and send it today. Hurry, darn it!"

Lucas sat reading in the library of his home in Kansas City. It had been a long time since he had done any reading and a lot of new information had arrived that might be helpful in his cattle business. He had expanded, taken over a ranch in Texas, and kept himself busy. He had just returned after a month to find the house as he had left it except for his mail. Katie had moved in with her sister, who was not able to care for herself anymore. He would miss her.

He stood and looked out across the trees and fields

behind his home. Autumn was here and the leaves were a foot thick on the ground. He would need to find somebody to clean up the yard. As he turned from the window he dropped the mail he was still holding.

His head still ached when he leaned over too far and the pain began its usual pounding as he reach to retrieve the letters and pamphlets scattered across the carpet. Just then the doorbell rang.

''Darned headaches!''

The bell rang again.

''I'm coming, hold it a minute.''

It was almost November. Agatha decided to go riding even though the morning air was quite cool. It would warm up as it did every day this time of year. Jubilee seemed to enjoy their rides up into the hills and would stand at the door to her stall waiting for Nate to put on her bridle and saddle. Then she knew Agatha was coming with a treat—a lump of sugar or an apple.

''Here she is, Miss Agatha.'' Nate had Jubilee ready.

''Thanks, Nate. Tell Clarisa I may be gone awhile today. I'm going up to the hill beyond the house and read for a while. Jubilee will enjoy a chance to graze, I'm sure.''

''Fine, you just take your time.''

Agatha got up into the saddle and rode the horse to the top of the hill where she and Lucas had spent that one wonderful evening—the night he first told her of his love.

A breeze touched Agatha's face, as gentle as silk. She had tethered Jubilee and was looking out across the valley at the face of the new Virginia City that was slowly being rebuilt. There was something wonderful about watching the earth and its people renew themselves. Life did go on in spite of the problems, the hurts, and death. The quiet of the moment was helping to give her some gentle comfort. She stretched out and started to read. She was so tired, so very, very tired. She put the book down and rested her head against the hillside and soon fell asleep.

The sun had moved across the sky until it finally dipped behind the highest mountain peak to the north. Its shadow cooled the spot where Agatha slept, and the chill finally woke her. The sky had clouded over and looked gray, as if a storm were brewing over the mountains in the west. It took her a moment to remember just where she was, and as she looked around she could see someone in the distance riding up from the manor. At first she thought it must be Nate, concerned about her long absence, but then she realized it could not be; the man on the horse was too tall, too big. Suddenly time stood still and everything around her seemed to stop moving. It couldn't be, but it was. It was Lucas. He rode the last short distance toward Agatha and pulled the mare up beside her. For a long moment he just sat and looked down into her face; then, reaching over with one arm, he pulled her up onto the saddle in front of him and rode ahead toward a stand of cottonwood trees. Only then did he stop, get off the horse, and lift her down to the ground.

"Don't say anything, please. Just let me look at you. It's been so long. I can't believe I'm here!"

With these words he folded her into his arms. His urgent kiss proved that he was real and alive. Until that moment Agatha thought she had been dreaming.

"There's so much I have to tell you, so much explaining to do."

"Lucas, not now. I knew that you would come back to me. Right now it is enough that you are here and we are together."

From the back veranda, Clarisa and Nate could see Lucas and Agatha standing beneath the cottonwood trees. Clarisa was crying and Nate was smiling.

A soft whispering rain passed over the mountains.